IN
DISA

'Ingenious puzzle'

The Times

'All told with a sophisticated coolness and lots of local knowledge of the seamier side of current theatrical life'

Birmingham Post

'Very funny, well characterised'

Sunday Telegraph

CAST, IN ORDER OF DISAPPEARANCE

Simon Brett

KEYHOLE CRIME
London · Sydney

*First published in Great Britain 1975 by
Victor Gollancz Ltd.*

*This edition published 1982 by
Keyhole Crime, 15–16 Brook's Mews,
London W1A 1DR*

ISBN 0 263 74027 7

Set in 10 on 11½ pt Linotron Times
06/0982

*Photoset by Rowland Phototypesetting Ltd
Bury St Edmunds, Suffolk
Made and printed in Great Britain by
Cox & Wyman Ltd, Reading*

TO LUCY

CONTENTS

CHAPTER ONE

CINDERELLA ALONE

'Charles, Charles love, it's your cue.'

Charles Paris jerked out of his doze. He looked down for the script on his knees, but *The Times* crossword with two completed clues stared blankly up at him. He dropped the paper, opened his script, and looked hopefully at the little actress next to him for the page number.

'Page 27, Line 4,' the producer snapped with all the exasperation of a large mortgage in Pinner and another nineteen years till his BBC pension.

'Sorry . . .' said Charles, trying to remember the producer's name. 'Sorry, love,' failing to do so.

He read his lines with leaden incomprehension. A twinge of guilt for having done no preparation soon passed when he heard the lines he was reading. Wasn't anyone writing good radio plays any more? As his scene ground to a halt, he looked across at the spindly raffia-haired youth responsible. The Author sat by the producer in a twisted attitude of intense concentration or bad piles. Every now and then he winced as another nuance of his writing was steamrollered.

The play reached its denouement with all the impact of a wet dishcloth, and there was a ripple of dejected laughter. 'Well,' said the producer, 'now the real work starts. But first let's send the lovely Sylvia for some tea.'

Charles took the opportunity to go to the Gents and lose lunchtime's excesses of wine. To his annoyance the Author joined him at the adjacent urinal. Charles resolutely pretended he hadn't noticed.

'Um, Charles . . .'

'Yes.'

'I hope you don't mind my saying . . .'

'No, of course not.'

'Well, I'd seen the Inspector rather Grand Guignol . . .'

'Ah.'

'And I thought you read him rather . . .'

'Yes . . . ?'

'Well, Petit Guignol.'

'Ah,' said Charles Paris. 'I'll try to do something about it.'

Even Arctic nights end, and so, somehow, did the day in the studio. Charles's performance, however Grand its Guignol, was fixed on tape. It all seemed to matter less as he stood in the BBC Club and the first large Bell's glowed inside him. It was December 3rd and the short walk from Broadcasting House to the Club had been breathtakingly cold after the recycled warmth of the studio.

Sherlock Forster (known to his intimates as Len) was an undemanding companion. A distinguished radio actor and a great piss-artist, he had been playing the murderer in the play and was now slumped against the bar, caressing a large Riesling, his toupée'd head deep into the *Evening Standard*. 'Hoarding outside said "Motorist Shot Dead." Thought it might have pushed the bloody Arabs out of the headlines,' he said to no one in particular.

'Did it?' asked Charles.

'No such luck. Main story's still bloody petrol queues. "Motorist Shot Dead" is way down the column.'

'Where'd it happen?'

'Just off the M4 somewhere. Apparently the bloke'd run out of petrol, got out of the car, and some bugger shot him.'

'Poor sod.'

'Police are treating it as a case of murder.'

'Shrewd of them. Anything else in the paper?'

'Well, the Archbishop of Canterbury's being driven round in a Morris Minor to save petrol. And a couple of Cabinet ministers turned up at the House in a Mini.'

'Chauffeur-driven, no doubt.'

The second large Bell's changed the glow within Charles to a feeling of positive well-being. Forty-seven years old and still attractive to women. The lack of matinée-idol good looks which had kept him from being a star in the Fifties was no longer a disadvantage. He had worn better than a lot of his contemporaries. Hair still grew thick and only lightly silvered at the temples. He looked at Len's theatrical toupée and felt grateful.

Life, Charles reflected, was not too bad. Even financially, for once. He was still flush from a ghastly television series in which he'd minced around some unlikely Tudor monarch in doublet and hose for a couple of months. And when he'd drunk through that money, or when the taxman caught up with him, something else would happen. He cast a professional eye round the bar. A few standard-issue BBC spinsters; one or two attractive younger secretaries, sentried by men; nothing worth chatting up.

'Petrol, bloody petrol,' said Len. 'There's nothing else in the paper. Look at this—"Attractive 19-year-old model Patti Winchester isn't worried. She's been showing a leg and riding her bicycle for months now."'

Charles glanced over. 'Tatty.'

'Hmm. Footballer Bobby Lithgoe has bought a bicycle too.'

'Wow.'

'And Marius Steen has put the Rolls in the garage.'

'Steen? What does it say about him?'

'"Impresario Marius Steen, the man behind such stage successes as *One Thing After Another, Who's*

Afraid of the Big Bed Wolf? and, of course, his current smash-hit at the King's Theatre, *Sex of One and Half a Dozen of the Other*, phoned today at his Berkshire home, said, 'We'll leave the Rolls in the garage and use the Datsun.'"'

'He's got a good publicity machine. It's just a straight plug for that bloody *Sex of One* . . .'

'Clocked up a thousand performances last week.'

'God. How revolting.'

'Big party on-stage at the King's on Saturday.'

'It'll probably run forever. There's no justice.' Charles picked up Len's empty glass. 'Another one of those?'

'Why not?'

Predictably the BBC Club had led to the George, the George to a small pub off Drury Lane, and at about mid-night Charles, having lost Len somewhere along the line, found himself leaning against a banister in the Montrose with a pint in his hand.

The Montrose (a small theatrical drinking club off the Haymarket) was full as usual. A lot of rooms on different levels, shoddy like converted bedsitters, overflowing with actors talking and gesturing loudly.

'. . . got a *Z-Cars* coming up. Small part, but nice . . .'

'. . . and he said to William, "You've got as much humour as a crutch!" She was furious . . .'

'. . . working towards a modern commedia format . . .'

'. . . ultimately it's a matter of identity . . .'

'Hello, Charles.' A voice detached itself from the rest and Charles focused on a small blonde girl in front of him. 'Jacqui.'

* * *

Jacqui had a top-floor flat in Archer Street, opposite a casino whose lights usually flashed yellow all night. But now with the power restrictions, they were dark. Only the blue glow of a solitary streetlamp touched their anaemic neon tubes. But there were still the noises of the casino—the hum and slam of taxis, the shouts of drunkards and the chatter of Chinese gamblers in the street below.

Charles looked at Jacqui with pleasure. She was an actress-cum-dancer-cum-most-things he'd met in pantomime at Worthing. He'd been Baron Hardup, Cinderella's father; and she had been a Villager, White Mouse and Court Lady (for the Finale). They'd had quite a pleasant time in Worthing. It was good to see her again.

But she looked upset. Charles filled his glass from the bottle of Southern Comfort and slumped back onto the white fur of the bed, shaking a small oil-lamp on the bedside table. 'And you can't get in touch with him?'

'No. I've tried both the houses. And the office.'

'I wouldn't worry, Jacqui. He'll call you.'

'Maybe.' She still looked tense and hurt. Strange, how a girl like that, who'd had everyone and done everything, could be so affected by one dirty old man not getting in touch with her. And Marius Steen of all people.

Jacqui stretched out her strong dancer's legs and stared at her toes. 'No. He often doesn't call for weeks on end. He's moody. Sometimes he doesn't want me around. I'm his secret vice. Just a tottie. I mean, if he's going to a do with the Queen Mum, he can't take a tart along.' Charles grunted uncomfortably. 'No, that's what I am. I don't really want to be more than that. He's an old man, he's nice to me, we have a few giggles, that's all. It couldn't possibly last. I know that.' She sounded as if she was bravely repeating a formula she didn't believe.

'When did you last see him?'

'Saturday afternoon.'

'For God's sake, what is it now? Only Monday. Give him a chance.'

'I know, but this time I think it's over.'

'Why?'

'When I rang, there was a message. Said I wasn't to contact him again.'

'Ah.'

Jacqui poured herself a large glass of Southern Comfort and took a savage swallow at it. 'Bugger him. I'm not going to get miserable about an old sod like that.' She rose and flopped down on the bed beside Charles. 'There are other men.'

'Still older men, I'm afraid.'

'You're not old.'

'I'm forty-seven.'

'That's cradle-snatching by my standards,' she said with a wry laugh. Then she stopped short. 'Old sod. It's all because of the knighthood.'

'Hmm?'

'His last ambition. Reckoned he might get one this New Year.'

'Services to the Theatre?'

'I suppose so. And I suppose I let down the image. Well, I don't care about him.' She snuggled up to Charles.

'Jacqui, am I being used merely for revenge? As a sex-object?'

'Yes. Any objections?'

'No.'

Charles kissed her gently. He felt protective towards her, as if she might suddenly break down.

Her tongue flickered round the inside of his mouth and they drew apart. 'You smell like a distillery,' she said.

'I am a distillery,' he replied fatuously and hugged her close to him. She had a comforting little body, and the smoky taste of her mouth was familiar. 'Hmm. We had a good time in Worthing. We were better than the dirty postcards.'

Jacqui smiled closely into his eyes and her hand fumbled for his zip. She couldn't find the little metal pull-tag. An exasperated breath. 'You know, Charles, I always think it's simpler to take your own things off. If you're both in agreement.'

'I'm in agreement,' said Charles. He rolled over to the side of the bed and fumblingly undressed. When he turned round, Jacqui was lying naked on the bed, familiar in the pale street light. 'Charles.'

'Must take my socks off. Otherwise I feel like an obscene photo.'

He lay down beside her and hugged her, warm on the fur. They held each other close, hands gliding over soft flesh.

After a few moments Charles rolled away. 'Not very impressive, am I?'

'Don't worry. It doesn't matter.'

'No.' A pause. 'Sorry. I'm not usually like this.'

'I know,' Jacqui said meaningfully. 'And I know what to do about it.'

He felt her moving, a soft kiss on his stomach, then the warmth of her breath as it strayed downwards. 'Jacqui, don't bother. I'm not in the mood. It's the booze or . . .'

'OK. Poor old Baron Hardup.'

'I'm sorry, Jacqui.'

'Don't worry. All I really need is a good cuddle.'

'Tonight I'm afraid that's all I can offer you.' And he hugged her very closely like a teddy bear in his arms. In a moment he had sunk into a heavy, but troubled sleep.

CHAPTER TWO

THE FAIRY GODMOTHER

As Charles walked past the manicured front gardens of Muswell Hill, he tried to piece together his feelings. It was a long time since he had been so churned up inside. For years life had jogged on from hangover to hangover, with the odd affair between drinks, and nothing had affected him much. But now he felt jumpy and panicky.

Impotence is perhaps not unusual in a man of forty-seven. And anyway it probably wasn't impotence, just the dreaded Distiller's Droop. Nothing to worry about.

But that wasn't the important part of his feelings. There was a change in his attitude to Jacqui. He felt an enormous need to protect the girl, as if, by failing in bed, he had suddenly become responsible for her. She seemed desperately vulnerable, like a child in a pram or an old man in a launderette. Perhaps these were paternal feelings, the sort he had somehow never developed for his daughter.

Together with this new warmth came the knowledge that he had to go and see Frances. 'Marriage,' Charles reflected wryly as he clicked open her wrought-iron gate, 'is the last refuge of the impotent.'

She wasn't there. Still at school. Not even six o'clock yet. Charles had a key and let himself in. His hand instinctively found the light-switch.

The house hadn't changed. As ever, a pile of books to be marked on the dining table, concert programmes, an old Edinburgh Festival brochure. Earnest paperbacks about psychology and sociology on the bookshelves. Auntie May's old upright piano with the lid up. And on top, that terrible posed photograph of Juliet with pigtails and a grim smile over the brace on her teeth. Next to it, the puzzle jug. Then that windswept snapshot of him, Charles Paris, taken on holiday on Arran. It was a real LP sleeve photograph. Better than any of that expensive rubbish he'd had done for *Spotlight*.

He resisted the temptation to raid the drinks cupboard, switched on the television and slumped into the sofa they'd bought at Harrods when flush from selling the film rights of his one successful play.

He heard the guarded voice of a newscaster, then the picture buzzed and swelled into life. The news was still dominated by petrol and the prospect of rationing. Charles couldn't get very excited about it.

Police had identified the motorist shot off the M4 at Theale. A blurred snapshot was blown up to fill the screen. It had the expression of a man already dead. There had been no petrol in the victim's car; the back right-hand wing was dented; he had been shot through the head and left by the roadside. Police were still trying to find a motive for the killing.

'In the second day of the Sally Nash trial at the Old Bailey, a 17-year-old girl, Miss C., told of sex-parties at London hotels. A lot of show-business people—' Charles switched over to the serious face of Eamonn Andrews talking to someone about petrol rationing. He switched again and got a sizzling snowstorm through which a voice imparted mathematical information.

'Sodding UHF.' He got down on his hands and knees in front of the box and started moving the portable aerial about. The snowstorm varied in intensity. Then he remembered the UHF contrast knob and went round the set to turn it.

'Television repair man.' He'd been too close to the sound to hear Frances come in.

'Hello.' He stood up. 'Look. The picture's perfect.'

'Are you doing an Open University degree?'

'No. I was just getting it right. It's the UHF contrast.'

'Ah.' She looked at him. 'How are you?'

'Bad.'

'I thought so. Do you want something to eat?'

'I don't know.'

'That means yes. Did you have lunch?'

'Pie in a pub.'

'Ugh.' Frances went into the kitchen and started opening cupboards. She continued talking through the serving hatch. It was restfully familiar.

'I went down to see Juliet and Miles at the weekend.'

'Ah.'

'Nice to get out of town.'

'Yes.'

'They said they'd love to see you. You should go down, it's a lovely place.'

'Yes. I will. At some stage. How's Miles?'

'Oh, he's doing very well.'

'Ah.' Charles visualised his son-in-law, Miles Taylerson, the rising executive, neat in his executive house on his executive estate in Pangbourne with his executive car and his executive suits and his executive haircut. 'Do you like Miles, Frances?'

'Juliet's very happy with him.'

'Which I suppose,' Charles reflected, 'is some sort of answer.' Thinking of his daughter made him think of Jacqui again and he felt a flutter of panic in his stomach.

Frances produced the food very quickly. It was a dish with frankfurters and sour cream. Something new. Charles felt jealous at the thought that she was developing, learning new things without him. 'Tell you what,' he said, 'shall I whip down to the off-licence and get a bottle of wine? Make an evening of it.'

'Charles, I can't make an evening of it.' I've got to be at a PTA meeting at 7:30.'

'Parents-Teachers? Oh, but can't you—' He stopped.

No, you can't come back to someone you walked out on twelve years ago and expect them to be instantly free. Even if you have kept in touch and had occasional reconciliations. 'Have a drink together later, maybe.'

'Maybe. If you're still here.'

'I will be.'

'What is the matter, Charles?'

'I don't know. Male menopause?' It was a phrase he'd read in a colour supplement somewhere. Didn't really know if it meant anything.

'You think you've got problems,' said Frances.

She was always busy. Two things about Frances—she was always busy and she was never surprised. These, in moments of compatibility, were her great qualities; in moments of annoyance, her most irritating traits.

The next morning she cooked a large breakfast, brought it up to him in bed, and hurried off to school. Charles lay back on the pillows and felt mellow. He saw the familiar gable of the Jenkinses opposite (they'd had the paintwork done blue) and felt sentimentality well up inside him. Each time he came back to Frances, he seemed to feel more sentimental. At first. Then after a few days they'd quarrel or he'd feel claustrophobic and leave again. And go on a blinder.

The impotence panic seemed miles away. It was another person who had felt that nausea of fear in his stomach. Long ago.

They had made love beautifully. Frances's body was like a well-read book, familiar and comforting. Her limbs were thinner, the tendons a bit more prominent and the skin of her stomach loose. But she was still soft and warm. They had made love gently and easily, their bodies remembering each other's rhythms. It's something you never forget, Charles reflected. Like riding a bicycle.

He switched on the radio by the bedside. It was tuned to Capital Radio—pop music and jingles. So that's what Frances listened to. Strange. It was so easy to condemn her as bourgeois and predictable. When you actually came down to it, everything about her was unexpected. What appeared to be passivity was just the great calm that emanated from her.

When he was dressed, he needed human companionship and so rang his agent. 'Maurice Skellern Artistes,' said a voice.

'Maurice.'

'Who wants him?'

'Maurice, I know that's you. It's me, Charles.'

'Oh, hello. How'd the radio go?'

'Ghastly. It was the worst script I've ever seen.'

'It's work, Charles.'

'Yes, just.'

'Were you rude to anybody?'

'Not very. Not as rude as I felt like being.'

'Who to?'

'The producer.'

'Charles, you can't afford it. Already you'll never get another job on *Doctor Who*.'

'I wasn't very rude. Anything coming up?'

'Some vacancies on the permanent company at Hornchurch.'

'Forget it.'

'Chance of a small part in a *Softly, Softly*.'

'Put my name up.'

'New play at one of these new fringe theatres. About transvestites in a prison. Political overtones. Written by a convict.'

'It's not really *me*, is it, Maurice?' in his best theatrical knight voice.

'I don't know what is *you* any more, Charles. I sometimes wonder if you want to work at all.'

'Hmm. So do I.'

'What are you living on at the moment?'

'My second childhood.'

'I don't get ten per cent of that.'

'No. What else is new?'

'Nothing.'

'Come on. Give us the dirt.'

'Isn't any. Well, except for the Sally Nash business . . .'

'Oh yes?'

'Well, you know who thc disc jockcy was, for a start . . . ?' And Maurice started. He was one of London's recognised authorities on theatrical gossip. Malicious rumour had it that he kept a wall-chart with coloured pins on who was sleeping with whom. The Sally Nash case gave him good copy. It was the Lambton affair of the theatre, complete with whips, boots, two-way mirrors and unnamed 'show-business personalities.' For half an hour Maurice named them all. Eventually, he rang off. That's why he was such a lousy agent. Spent all his time gossiping.

By the Thursday morning Charles's mellowness felt more fragile. When he woke at nine, Frances had already gone to school. He tottered downstairs and made some coffee to counteract the last night's Beaujolais. The coffee tasted foul. Laced with Scotch, it tasted better. He drank it down, poured a glass of neat Scotch and went upstairs to dress.

The inside of his shirt collar had dark wrinkles of dirt, and his socks made their presence felt. Soon he'd have to get Frances to wash something or go back to Hereford Road and pick up some more clothes.

He sloped back downstairs. Frances's *Guardian* was neatly folded on the hall chest. No time to read it at school. Organised read in the evening. It had to be the *Guardian*.

Charles slumped on to the Harrods sofa and started reading an article on recycling waste paper. It failed to hold his attention. He checked the television times and switched on *Play School*. The picture was muzzy. He started fiddling with the UHF contrast knob. The phone rang.

'Hello.'

'Charles.'

'Jacqui. Where on earth did you get this number?'

'You gave it me ages ago. Said you were contactable there in the last resort.'

'Yes. I suppose it is my last resort. What's up?'

'It's about Marius.'

'Yes?'

'I tried to contact him again. Went to the house in Bayswater. It was a stupid thing to do, I suppose. Should've left him alone. Should be able to take a bloody hint. I don't know.'

'What happened?'

'He wasn't there. But this morning I had a letter.'

'From Marius?'

'Yes. It wasn't signed, but it must be. It's horrid. Charles, I'm shit-scared.'

'Shall I come round?'

'Can you?'

'Yes.' A pause. 'Why did you ring me, Jacqui?'

'Couldn't think of anyone else.'

After he had put the phone down, Charles switched off *Play School*. He took an old envelope from the table and wrote on it in red felt pen, 'THANKS. GOODBYE. SEE YOU.' Then he left the house and set out for Highgate tube station.

CHAPTER THREE

WHO WAS AT THE BALL?

Charles looked at the sheet of paper. It was pale blue with a dark bevelled edge and, on it, scrawled in black biro capitals, was an uncompromising message. Basically, it told Jacqui to get lost when she wasn't wanted. And basically was the way it was done. The language was disgusting and the note anonymous. 'Charming. Are you sure it's from him?'

'No one else had any reason.'

'And is the language in character?'

'Yes, he never was very delicate. Particularly when he was angry. Could be quite frightening.'

'Paper familiar?'

'Yes. He had it on his desk at Orme Gardens. Some headed, some plain like this.'

'Hmm. Well, there's only one way to treat shit of this sort.' Charles screwed the note up into a dark glass ashtray and set it on fire with the table lighter. When the flame had gone, he blew the black ash carefully into the wastepaper basket. 'When did it come?'

'It was on the mat when I got up. About eleven. A bit after.'

'Come by post?'

'No. Plain envelope. On the table.'

Charles leant over and picked it up. Blue, matching the paper. Told him nothing. 'And I suppose you didn't . . . ?'

'See anyone? No.'

'It's a fairly nasty way of breaking something off, isn't it?'

'Yes.' She looked near to tears. 'And I thought it was going so well.'

'Perhaps he's just a nasty man.'

'He could be, I know. But with me he was always kind. When we were in France, he—'

'When was this?'

'We went in August, came back in October. Marius's got a villa down the South. Sainte-Maxime. It's a lovely place. Private beach.'

'Very nice.'

'Anyway, he took me there to recuperate.'

'What from?'

'I'd had an abortion.'

'His baby?'

'Yes. He fixed it up, but it didn't quite go right. I was ill. So he took me out to Sainte-Maxime.'

'And he was there all the time?'

'Yes. He'd been ill too—had a minor heart-attack. He was meant to be resting, though, of course, being Marius, he was in touch with the office every day.'

'It was just the two of you out there?'

'Mostly. Some friends of his dropped in, theatre people. And Nigel for a bit.'

'Nigel?'

'His son.'

'Oh, yes.' Charles remembered someone once mentioning that Steen had a son. 'I didn't think they got on.'

'That was ages ago. They made it up, more or less. Nigel works in the business.'

'And while you were out in France, it was all OK? Between you and Marius?'

'Yes. We had a marvellous time. He was very silly and childish. And kind.'

'And now he sends you notes like that. You can't think of any reason for the change in his attitude?'

Jacqui hesitated. 'No. Would you like some lunch?'

While she cooked, Charles went down to the off-licence and bought a bottle of wine. It was obvious from Jacqui's manner that she did have an idea why Steen had changed. And that she was going to tell him. It was only a matter of waiting.

The lunch was unremarkable. Jacqui was a frozen food cook. He remembered it from Worthing. Endless beefburgers and cod steaks with bright peas and diced vegetables. But the wine made it passable. They talked back to Worthing, hedging round the subject of Steen. Eventually, as Charles drained the bottle evenly into their two glasses, he asked, 'What do you want me to do, Jacqui?'

'What do you mean?'

'You've brought me round here for a reason.'

'I was frightened.'

'Yes, but there's something else.'

'Yes.' She looked very vulnerable. Again he felt the sense of debt that had started when he failed her in bed. The contract was unfulfilled. If he could not serve her in one way, he would serve her in another. It's strange, he thought, is this what chivalry's come to?

'I do want you to do something for me, Charles. It's sort of awkward. You see, I think I know . . . I think I might know why Marius is behaving like this. He might think . . . you see . . .' Charles bided his time. Jacqui looked at him directly and said, 'You've heard of all this Sally Nash business?'

'Yes. Is Marius involved in that?'

'Not really. Not with the prostitutes. It's just . . . well, she, Sally Nash, used to be at some parties that we went to.'

'Just ordinary parties?'

'Well . . .' Jacqui smiled sheepishly. 'No, not ordinary parties really. Things happened.'

'I didn't know that was your scene. I thought you only

slept with one man at a time and . . .' Charles tailed off, embarrassed.

'No, it's not my sort of thing. But Marius was into all that. Only a bit. Nothing very serious.'

'Hmm.'

'Don't sound so bloody superior. It's easy for a man. If you're a girl you have to get interested in what your bloke's interested in. If he's mad on football, you watch *Match of the Day*. If it's two-way mirrors, well . . .'

'Was it like that in the South of France?'

'No. It was only a couple of times we ever did it. Last June. There was a party in Holland Park, and one near Marble Arch.'

'But they were Sally Nash's parties?'

'She was there.'

'And what's the danger? Are you going to be called as a witness?'

'Bloody hell.' She looked very affronted. 'Look, I may be a tart, but I'm not a whore.' Charles tried vaguely to work out the distinction, but fortunately Jacqui clarified. 'All these girls they're calling in the trial do it for money.'

'I'm sorry. Then what's the . . . ?'

'There are some photographs.'

'Of you and Steen at the party?'

'Yes. With some other people.'

'Naughty photos?'

'A bit naughty. But I think that's why Marius doesn't want to be seen with me.'

'Why? Are the photographs going to come up in court?'

'No, they aren't. But Marius must think they will. It's the only explanation.'

'But if you're both in the photos, he could be identified anyway. It doesn't make any difference whether he's seen with you or not.'

'No, Charles. The point is, they can't tell it's him. His face is covered.'

'Don't tell me—with a black leather mask.'

'Yes.'

'Really? I was joking.'

'Well, it is.'

'But you, on the other hand, are not covered?'

'No. Far from it.'

'Hmm. How do you know they won't come up in court?'

'Because I've got them. I paid a lot of money for them.'

'Did someone blackmail you?'

'No. The Sally Nash trial started on Friday, and I bought them off the bloke who took them on Saturday.'

'How much?'

'Thousand quid.'

Charles looked at her quizzically and she explained. 'Marius had given me some money to buy a car, but it hardly seems worth buying one now, with all this petrol scene.'

Charles reflected momentarily on the difference between a tart and a whore and decided he was being a bit harsh. Particularly as Jacqui continued, 'I wanted to give them to Marius as a present. Set his mind at rest. And now I can't get to see him. I daren't send them through the post or letter-box, because his secretary'll see them . . .'

Suddenly Charles's role in the proceedings became very clear to him. 'And so you want me to deliver them?'

Armed with an innocuous-looking brown envelope, Charles Paris returned to his room in Hereford Road, Bayswater. It was a depressing furnished bedsitter, which he'd moved into when he left Frances. Nothing except his clothes and scripts gave it any identity. The furniture had been painted grey by some earlier occupant, but was mostly obscured by drip-dry shirts on wire hangers. A low upholstered chair with wooden arms sat in front of the gas-fire. There was a small table covered with paper and carbons, a rickety kitchen chair, a single bed shrouded in yellow candlewick, and in one corner, inadequately hidden by plastic curtain, a sink and gas-ring.

Whenever Charles entered the room, fumes of depression threatened to choke him. Every now and then, in a surge of confidence, he would consider moving, but he never got round to it. The room was somewhere to sleep and he did his best to ensure that that was all he did there.

He got back about five and, before the atmosphere of the room had time to immobilise him, opened the cupboard, got out a half-full bottle of Bell's and poured himself a healthy measure. After a substantial swallow, he felt he could look at his surroundings. It was more of a mess than usual. Candlewick in disarray on the unmade bed, coffee cup with a white crust on the table. Cold December air was gushing through the open window. He remembered leaving it to air the place on . . . when was it? Monday? Yes, Monday, 3rd December. The day he'd done that bloody awful radio play.

He slammed the window and put on the gas-fire. It hissed resentfully but came alight (which was more than it sometimes did). He felt strongly in need of a bath, stripped off his grubby clothes and put on a shapeless towelling dressing-gown. Taking a fivepence from his change, he went down to the bathroom on the first landing, checked that the water wasn't running hot, and fed the meter.

Then he remembered soap and towel. Upstairs again to get them. Inevitably, the bathroom door was locked when he returned. The sound of running water came from inside.

Charles hammered on the door and shouted abuse, but the strange sing-song voice that replied over the sound of water told him it was useless. One of the Swedish girls. There seemed to be hundreds of them in the house. And, he thought as he savagely stumped upstairs, all of them old boots. They really shattered the myth of Scandinavian beauty, that lot. Spotty girls with glasses and rugger-players' legs. He slammed the door, picked up the whisky bottle and fell into the chair.

The gas-fire spluttered at him as he sat and thought. There was something odd about the whole business with Jacqui. Her explanation about the photographs seemed unconvincing. In fact, her account of Steen's sudden change of behaviour didn't ring true either. A man in his position who wanted to get rid of a girlfriend needn't go to the length of obscene notes.

For a moment the thought crossed Charles's mind that he was being used in some sort of plot. To carry something. What? Drugs? Or just what Jacqui said it was—dirty pictures? But it seemed ridiculous. A much simpler explanation was that she was telling the truth.

The way to find out, of course, was to look in the envelope. He'd known since he had had the photographs that sooner or later he would. And, he reasoned, Jacqui must have assumed he would. She hadn't asked him not to; the envelope was unsealed. But he still felt slightly guilty as he shuffled them into his hand.

There were six, and they were exactly what Jacqui had said they would be—obscene pictures of her and Marius Steen. Perhaps obscene was the wrong word; they didn't have any erotic effect on Charles; but they intrigued and rather revolted him.

The photographs had the posed quality of amateur dramatics. Steen's body was old, a thin belly and limbs like a chicken's. The tatty little leather mask made him look ridiculous. But, Charles was forced to admit, the old man was rather well endowed.

But it was the sight of Jacqui that affected him. There she was in a series of contrived positions—astride Steen, bending down in front of him, under him on a bed. The sight was a severe shock to Charles; it made him feel almost sick. Not the acts that were going on; he'd seen and done worse, and somehow they seemed very mild and meaningless on these shoddy little snapshots. But it was the fact that it was Jacqui which upset him. He didn't feel jealousy or lust, but pity and again the urgent desire to protect her. It was as if he was seeing the photographs as her father.

A click and silence told him that the gas meter had run out. Blast, he hadn't got a ten p. Brusquely, he shoved the photographs back into the envelope, sealed it and dressed. Then he started his campaign to get to see Marius Steen. It was half past seven. He went to the call box on the landing and rang up Bernard Walton, currently starring in *Virgin on the Ridiculous* at the Dryden Theatre.

CHAPTER FOUR

PRINCE CHARMING

George, the stage doorman at the Dryden Theatre, looked at him suspiciously. 'What's your name?'

'Charles Paris. Mr Walton is expecting me.'

George's face registered total disbelief and he turned to the telephone. Charles wondered vaguely if the old man had recognised him. After all, he'd come in every night for eighteen months during the run of *The Water Nymph* only ten years before. But no, the name Charles Paris meant nothing. So much for the showbiz myth of the cheery old 'never forget a face—I seen 'em all' doorman. George was a bloody-minded old sod and always had been.

'Mr Walton's not back in his dressing-room yet.'

'I'll wait.' Charles leaned against the wall. The doorman watched his visitor as if he expected him to steal the light fittings.

There was a big poster of the show stuck up just inside the stage door. It had on it an enormous photo of Bernard in hot pursuit of a cartoon of two bikini-clad girls. That's stardom—a real photo; supports only get cartoons.

Charles thought back to when he'd first met Bernard in Cardiff—a gauche, rather insecure young man with a slight stammer. Even then he'd been pushy, determined to make it. Charles had been directing at the time and cast him as Young Marlowe in *She Stoops to Conquer*. Not a good actor, but Charles made him play himself and it worked. The stammer fitted Marlowe's embarrassment and Bernard got a very good press. A couple of years round the reps playing nervous idiots, then a television series, and now, entering his second year in *Virgin on the Ridiculous*, nauseating the critics and wowing the coach parties.

'Could you try him again?' George acquiesced grudgingly. This time he got through. 'Mr Walton, there's a Mr—what did you say your name was?'

'Charles Paris.'

'A Mr Charles Paris to see you. Oh. Very well.' He put the phone down. 'Mr Walton's expecting you.' In tones of undisguised surprise. 'Dressing-room One. Down the—'

But Charles knew the geography of the theatre and strode along the corridor. He knocked on the door and it was thrown open by Bernard, oozing bonhomie from a silk dressing-gown. 'Charles, dear boy. Lovely to see you.'

Dear boy? Charles balked slightly at that and then he realised that Bernard actually thought himself Noël Coward. The whole star bit. 'Good to see you, Bernard. How's it going?'

'Oh, *comme ci, comme ça*. Audience love it. Doing fantastic business, in spite of all the crisis, or whatever it's called. So I can't complain. I'm just opening a bottle of champagne if you . . .'

'Do you have any Scotch?'

'Sure. Help yourself. Cupboard over there.'

'Bernard. I've come to ask you a favour.' May as well leap straight in.

'Certainly. What can I do for you?'

'You know Marius Steen, don't you?'

'Yes, the old sod. He owns half this show. You know, if Marius Steen didn't exist, it would be necessary to invent him.'

Aphorisms too, thought Charles. Noël Coward has a lot to answer for. Generations of actors who, without a modicum of the talent, have pounced on the mannerisms.

'The thing is, I want an introduction to him.' At that moment, the door burst open and Margaret Leslie sparkled into the room, her tiny frame cotton-woolled in a great sheepskin coat. 'Maggie darling!' Bernard enveloped her in his arms. 'Darling, do you know Charles Paris? Charles, have you met Maggie?'

'No, I haven't actually, but I've admired your work for a long time.' Charles could have kicked himself for the cliché. It was truc, though. She was a brilliant actress and deserved her phenomenal success.

'Charles Paris?' she mused huskily. 'Didn't you write that awfully clever play *The Rate-payer*?' Charles acknowledged it rather sheepishly. 'Oh, I'm enchanted to meet you, Charles. I did it in rep. once. Played Wanda.'

'Glenda.'

'Yes, that's right.'

'Charles was an incredible help to me at the beginning of my career,' said Bernard with professional earnestness. 'I would have got nowhere without him. But nowhere.'

Charles felt diminished by the compliment. He'd have preferred Bernard to say nothing rather than patronise him. It was the gratitude of the star on *This Is Your Life* thanking the village schoolmaster who had first taken him to the theatre.

'Charles was just asking me about Marius.'

'Oh God,' said Maggie dramatically and laughed.

This put Charles on the spot. He didn't mind asking Bernard a favour on his own, but it was awkward with Maggie there.

'You said you wanted an introduction?' Bernard prompted.

Nothing for it. He'd have to go on. 'Yes. I . . . er . . .' he'd got the story prepared but it was difficult with an audience. 'I've written a new play. Light comedy. Thought it might be Steen's sort of thing.'

'Oh, I see. And you want me to introduce you, so that you can try and sell it to him.'

'Yes.' Charles felt humiliated. He'd never have sunk to this if he were actually trying to sell one of his plays. But it was the only possible approach to Steen he could think of. 'I hope you don't mind my asking . . .'

'No. Of course not. Old pals act. Happy to oblige.' And Bernard was. He was the great star and here was an old friend, less successful, wanting to be helped out. Charles winced at the thought of what he was doing. 'Is it urgent, dear boy?'

'It is a bit. There's an American agent nibbling.'

'Ah.' Bernard's tone didn't believe it. 'Well, you leave it with me, old chum. Have I got your number?'

Charles wrote it down. Margaret Leslie, who was wandering restlessly round the room, picked up a script from a table. 'Is this the new telly, Bernard?'

'Yes, it's awful. Not a laugh in it. I do get a bit sick of the way they keep sending me scripts to make funny. Here's a new show—may not be much good—never mind, book Bernard Walton, he'll get a few laughs out of it. I probably could, but I should get a bit of support from the script-writers. You ought to write something for me, Charles,' he added charmingly.

'Not really my style, Bernard.'

'Oh, I don't know.'

'Bernard,' Maggie hinted, 'I think we ought to . . .'

'Lord, yes. Is that the time? Charles, we're going out to eat. Why not join us? Going to the Ivy. Miles'll be there, John and Prunella, and Richard, I expect. I'm sure they could make room for another.'

Charles refused politely. He couldn't stomach an evening of bright showbiz back-chat. Outside the theatre he gulped great lungfuls of cold night air, but it didn't cleanse him inside. He still felt sullied by what he'd have to do—to crawl to someone like Bernard Walton.

There was only one solution. He hailed a cab and went to the Montrose. If he couldn't lose the feeling, perhaps he could deaden it.

A tremendous hammering at the door. Charles rolled out of bed and groped his way over to open it. One of the Swedish girls was standing there in a flowered nylon dressing-gown. Charles had time to register that she looked like a dinky toilet-roll cover before his head caught up with him. It felt as if it had been split in two by a cold chisel and someone was grinding the two halves together.

'Telephone.' The Swedish girl flounced off. Charles tried to make it down the stairs with his eyes closed to allay the pain. He felt for the receiver and held it gingerly to his ear. 'Hello?'

'Charles, I've done it!' Bernard's voice sounded insufferably cheerful. Charles grunted uncomprehending. 'I've spoken to Marius.'

'Ah.'

'Well, I haven't actually spoken to him, but I spoke to Joanne—that's his secretary—and I've fixed for you to see him this afternoon at four. That's if he's back. Apparently he's been down at Streatley since the weekend, but Joanne says he should be back today. Got some charity dinner on.'

'Look, Bernard, I . . . er . . .' Charles's smashed brain tried to put the words together. 'Thanks very . . . I . . . er . . . don't know how—'

'Don't mention it, dear boy.' Bernard's voice sounded as if it were opening a fête, big-hearted and patronising. 'Do you know Marius's office?'

'No. I—'

'Charing Cross Road. Milton Buildings. Just beyond the Garrick.'

'Ah. Look, I . . .'

'My dear fellow, not a word. I just hope it does you some good. Always glad to oblige. You helped me in the early days. Eh?'

If anything could have made Charles feel sicker, it was Bernard's bonhomie.

By quarter to four the pain in his head had subsided to a dull ache. He found Milton Buildings in Charing Cross Road without too much difficulty, though the entrance was narrow, shuffled between a café and a bookshop.

Inside, however, the buildings were spacious. The board downstairs carried an impressive list of theatrical impresarios, agents and lawyers. 'Marius Steen Productions' was on the second floor. Charles travelled up in the old-fashioned cage lift. The envelope in his inside pocket seemed to bulge enormously. He felt as he had in Oxford, the first time had had taken a girl out with a packet of French letters in his wallet. He remembered the sense of an obscene lump under his blazer, revealing his intentions to the entire university. Didn't know why he'd bothered. Virginal Vera, besotted with phonetics. Middle English and nothing else. The time that one wasted. He felt a twinge of embarrassment for the gaucheness of his youth.

'ENQUIRIES' and an arrow in gold leaf on the wall. It pointed to a panelled oak door. Charles knocked. 'Come in.'

A secretary was sitting behind a solid Victorian desk. This must be Joanne. Unmarried, about forty, but not the standard over-made-up spinster secretary. She looked very positive and rather attractive in a forbidding way. Unmarried by choice, not default. She rose to meet him. 'You must be Mr Paris.'

'Yes.'

'I thought I recognised you from the television.'

'Ah!' There's no answer to that, but it's gratifying.

'Mr Paris, I'm so sorry. I would have tried to contact you, but I hadn't a phone number. I'm afraid Mr Steen hasn't come up from the country.'

'Oh dear.'

'Yes, I'm sorry. I thought he'd be back today. It appears that he's reading some scripts and . . .'

'Oh, that's all right.'

'There's no one else who could help? Mr Cawley deals with a lot of the management side.'

'No, I don't think so.'

'Or Mr Nigel Steen should be in town later. He'll certainly be here over the weekend.'

'Has he been down at Streatley?'

'He went down yesterday. Perhaps he could . . . ?'

'No, no thanks, I wanted to see Mr Marius Steen personally.'

'Ah. Well, I'm sorry. I explained to Mr Walton that . . .'

'Yes. Don't worry.'

'Perhaps you could let me have your number and then I'll give you a call when Mr Steen is back in town and we could fix another appointment.'

'Yes.'

So that was it. Charles left the office with his pocketful of pornography, feeling flat. He wandered along the Charing Cross Road, trying to think what to do next, Galahad on hearing that someone else had found the Holy Grail, Knight Errant without an errand. He rang Jacqui from Leicester Square tube station and reported his lack of progress.

'You say he's in Streatley now?'

'Yes.'

'And Nigel's coming up to town?'

'Probably, but, Jacqui, don't try to contact him. Leave it to me. I'll get in touch with him after the weekend.'

'Yes . . .' Wistful.

'I'll sort it out, Jacqui.'

'Yes . . .' Drab.

Charles wandered aimlessly through Leicester Square to Piccadilly. A cartoon cinema was offering Tom and Jerry and Chaplin shorts. He hovered for a moment, but his mind was too full to be sidetracked. He had to find out more about Marius Steen. So he went down the steps to Piccadilly Underground station and bought a ticket for Tower Hill.

CHAPTER FIVE

SPECIALITY ACT

The Old People's Home was designed for daylight. Plate glass welcomed the sun in to warm the inmates who sat in armchairs, waiting. But now it was dark. The nurse hadn't been round yet to close the curtains and Charles Paris and Harry Chiltern looked out on galvanised frames of blackness. The offices around were empty and dead, street lights in the backwater thought unnecessary in the emergency. The windows seemed more forbidding than walls.

'I saw some programme on the television the other day,' said Harry after a moment's musing. 'All the club comics it was. Just telling gags. Terrible. No technique. Or do I mean all the same technique? I tell you, I've seen more variety in a tin of sardines.

'They don't have variety now. Not even the word. Variety with a big V. Used to mean something. No, I rang a mate in the Variety department at the BBC. Couple of years back, this was. He said, it's not Variety any more, it's Light Entertainment. Light Entertainment—now that's a different thing altogether.

'I mean, when Lennie and I done our act, we worked on it. Worked hard. A few gags, monologue—that was Lennie's bit—a few more gags, I'd do my drunk routine, and finish with a song and a bit of tap. I mean, rehearsed. Not just standing up there telling some joke you heard from a man in a pub. It was an act. People who come to see the Chiltern Brothers knew they'd get a real show. Get their money's worth. No, this television, I don't hold with it. Entertainment in your living room. That's not the place for entertainment—it's for your knitting and your eating and your bit of slap and tickle. You gotta go out—that's part of the entertaining. Make a night of it, eh?'

'Yes. I suppose the television's on all the time here.'

'From the moment it starts. Some of the old biddies stuck in front all day long, watching—I don't know—how to speak Pakistani, or what kiddies can do with a cotton-reel. All bleeding day long. I tell you, there's one old cripple, ugly old bird—more chins than a Chinese telephone directory—sits there nodding away at the testcard when it's on, doesn't notice. Mind you, it's a lot more interesting than some of the programmes, eh?'

Harry Chiltern cackled with laughter and subsided into silence as the nurse at last arrived to draw the curtains. 'Evening, Mr Chiltern.'

'Evening.'

'I see we've got a visitor. Hello.' The nurse smiled conspiratorially at Charles. Harry contemplated his highly polished shoes until she had left the room. 'Silly old cow. Thinks we're all gaga. "I see we've got a visitor." Who's we, eh? Apart from Georgie Wood, eh?' He laughed again, then stopped suddenly. 'Come on.' He eased himself out of the chair.

'What?'

'She's off now, doing the other curtains. We can whip down to the Bricklayers for a pint.'

'Should you?'

'Bloody hell, Charles. If I'm going to snuff it, I'd rather snuff it with a pint in my fist than one of their bloody mugs of Ovaltine. Come on.'

The Bricklayers' Arms was one of those modern pubs that capture all the atmosphere of an airport lounge. Hanging red lights shone on leatherette couches and framed relief pictures of vintage cars. Pop music pounded from the jukebox.

Still, it was a pub, and a pint. Harry seemed to appreciate it. He took a long swig, put the glass down and wiped his mis-shaven upper lip contentedly. Charles thought it might be the moment. 'Harry, I wanted to ask you about Marius Steen.'

'Oh yeah. Old Flash Steenie. Why?'

'I'm going to see him about a play I have written.' The lie slipped out easily enough. 'What's he like?' Harry didn't seem to react. 'You knew him round the halls, didn't you?'

'Oh yes. Just thinking about him. Steenie. Tough old bugger.'

'Where did he come from?'

'Poland, I think, originally. His parents come over in—I don't know—early twenties, I suppose. When Marius was about fifteen. He done all kinds of things in the business. I mean all kinds. Wrestling promotions, girlie shows, Variety. I think he even been on the boards himself in the early days. Yes, he was. Never saw him, but I heard he was terrible. Even says so himself, I think. He did a whistling act, maybe. Or speciality of some sort. Fire-eating perhaps it was? Hey, d'you hear about the fire-eater who couldn't go anywhere without meeting an old flame? Eh? Made him feel really hot under the collar.' Harry chuckled. 'Made that one up, y'know. Didn't have any of this script-writer nonsense in my day. You did your own act, and it was yours all the way. Yes.' He gazed absently ahead, and raised his glass to his lips with a trembling hand. Charles feared he might have to prompt again. But the old man continued.

'I first met Steenie at . . . where? Chiswick Empire, I think it was. Me and Lennie was some way down the bill and Steenie was managing this tap-dance act, as I recall. Think it was that. I don't know. He'd always got so many acts going.'

'All Variety stuff?'

'Oh, yes. Didn't do none of your Oh-my-Gawd theayter till after the war—second big job, you know. No, he was going round the halls, picking up the odd act, putting shows on, making money. Making money. Always knew where every penny was. Tight as a bottle-top. You hear him squeak every time he moves.'

'What was he like?'

'I don't know how to answer that. Hard as nails. A real bugger, particularly about money. Made a lot of enemies.'

'What sort of people?'

'People who hadn't read the small print of their contracts. Never missed a trick, old Steenie. I remember, one bloke, mind-reader he was—Steenie booked him for some Variety bill, forget where it was now. Anyway, opens first night—this mind-reader comes on—audience really gives him the bird. Lots of audiences were like that. Mind you, Lennie and I could usually get them round. Lennie had this thing, when the act was going bad, he'd . . . ah, Lennie—God rest his soul. Got them wetting themselves up on the clouds, I daresay . . .

'Anyway, this mind-reader act got the real bum's rush, no question. So Steenie sacks him. Fair enough, that's what you'd expect. But Steenie doesn't pay him nothing. Some let-out he'd got in the contract. Bloke may have been able to read minds, but he couldn't read a bleeding contract. Eh? Mind-reader got quite nasty. Tried to do old Steenie over.'

'What happened?'

'Not a lot. Steenie had Frank with him.'

'Frank?'

'Don't know what his real name was. Everyone called him Frank after Frankenstein—you know, the old monster. He was Polish and all, I think. Probably had some unpronounceable name. Ex-wrestler.'

'A sort of body-guard?'

'That's the idea. Steenie needed one of them, the way he done business.'

'Did he ever do anything illegal?'

'Ah, what's illegal? He was no more illegal than most of the fixers in this business. If you mean, could the law have got him, no. He'd never do nothing himself but, you know, things might happen. Frank was a big boy to have lean on you.'

'Is he still around?'

'Frank? No, he must be dead. Or shovelled off into the Old Folks like me. One of those big muscle-bound Johnnies. Go to fat when they stop training. Die of heart failure, most of them.'

'Do you reckon Steen would have found a replacement?'

'I don't know. He'd got a well-developed sense of self-protection, you know, always carried a gun in the glove-pocket of the car. Probably got another bruiser after Frank. But perhaps you don't need that sort of thing in the old lee-gitimate theayter. Only thing you have to look out for is the nancy-boys, eh?'

They laughed. Harry looked into his glass as if he could see for miles and Charles nudged him back on to the subject. 'Do you know Steen's son?'

'Nigel, isn't it?'

'That's right.'

'Yeah, I met him. Nasty bit of work. Oh, nothing criminal. Just a bit slimy. Often happens. Old man does well and the kids don't quite make it. I don't suppose you'd remember old Barney Beattie. Vent act. Dummy called Buckingham. Barney and Buckingham. Great they were. Barney, he had these two sons—tried to set up a song and dance act. Nothing. Nothing there. Hooked off every stage in the British Isles, they was. It happens like that.' The old man drained his pint reflectively.

'Can I get you another one, Harry?'

'No, it's my throw.'

'Oh, but I'll . . .'

'I can still pay my way.' And with dignity he took the two glasses over to the bar. He looked small in the crush and it was some time before the order got through. Then he returned, face contorted with concentration as he tried to keep the glasses steady in his blotched hands.

'There.' With triumph. 'Put hairs on your chest, Charlie.'

'Thanks.'

'Now, where were we? Yes. Steenie's boy. Ain't got the old man's talent, none of it. Been involved in one or two real disasters. You know, putting on drag shows, that sort of spectacle. But he ain't got the touch. Old Steenie, he'd make money out of a kid's conker match; Nigel'd close *The Mousetrap* within a week.'

'Do they get on?'

'Father and son? God knows. Sometimes they do, sometimes they don't. Great arguments, old man used to keep disowning the boy. Then they'd be as thick as thieves again. He likes all the family bit, Steenie. Wife died—oh, years ago, so the boy matters a lot. Jews are like that, aren't they?'

'Yes.'

'You want to know a lot about them, don't you?'

'Just interest.'

'Yes.' A pause. 'You know, Charlie my boy, from the way you says that I can tell what you really want is the dirt. All right then—' he edged closer so that he was whispering rather than shouting over the jukebox '—here's the nastiest rumour I've ever heard about Steenie—really nasty rumour. Dancer he knew—she was on a bill with me and Lennie down the Hackney

Empire. Steenie was putting the show on, and he'd got a thing going with this bint Veronica. Always put it about a bit, Steenie. Had a lot of lead in his pencil, that boy'—the image of the photographs flashed across Charles's mind—'Anyway, this girl gets knocked up, and when Steenie finds out about it, he don't want to know. Won't talk to her, doesn't know her, gives her the boot. Out of the show.

'Well, this Veronica won't put up with this—comes round the theatre between shows one night—really drunk—really—I don't like that in a woman—and she's swearing and effing and blinding—big shout-up with Steenie—going to tell his wife, all that. Next morning she's found floating face-down in the Thames.

'All right. Could have fallen in. Could have decided to do away with herself. But nasty rumours at the time said she could have been helped in. Certainly her being off the scene was handy for Steenie. And Frank wasn't round the theatre the night she disappeared. It's a long time ago, though. Just rumours.'

'Do you think Steen would be capable of that sort of thing, Harry?'

'If someone was in his way, Charlie, he'd be capable of anything.'

'I see, a real bastard.'

There was a long pause. 'Yes, a real bastard.' Harry chuckled. 'But you can't help liking him. One of the most likeable lumps of shit I ever come across.'

They talked a bit more, but Harry was tiring quickly. He seemed to be having difficulty with the second pint, and had only drunk a third of it when he looked at his watch. 'Better be on my way, you know, Charlie. Not as young as I was.'

'Will there be trouble when you get back?'

'No. I'll pretend I've had a turn or something. Ah, you know, I don't like that place. Still, not for long.'

'Are you moving somewhere else?'

Harry smiled. 'Join Lennie. Won't be long now. Still, can't complain.'

'A whole lifetime in the business.'

'Yes. Did our first show when we was four. And our last one three years ago on some stupid television thing about the music-hall. Seventy-four years in the business, that was, Charlie. Seventy-four.'

'And you wouldn't have had it any other way.'

'Good God, yes. It was Lennie who wanted all that. I wanted to be a professional footballer.'

CHAPTER SIX

TRANSFORMATION SCENE

Charles tried to think it all out on the Saturday morning. He'd woken without a hangover and even done a token tidying-up of his room. Then out for a newspaper and some rolls, and he was sitting in front of the gas-fire with a cup of coffee. Glance at the paper; no particular interest in petrol queues or Ireland without Whitelaw, so he settled down to think about Jacqui and Steen.

What he had heard from Harry Chiltern was disturbing. True, the business about the dancer in the Thames sounded a bit too melodramatic—the kind of story that gets embroidered over the years—and probably started out just as an unfortunate coincidence. Charles discounted the facts of it; but it was significant that Marius Steen attracted that sort of accusation. It didn't bode well for Jacqui.

Then there were the photographs and her own story. Something didn't ring true there. He pieced it together. In June, Jacqui and Steen went to a party, which was attended by Sally Nash, now on trial at the Old Bailey on charges of controlling prostitutes. At this party a fairly insipid orgy took place. Some pictures were taken by a nameless photographer. All through this period (according to Jacqui) things were swinging between her and Steen. She even got pregnant by him. He arranged an abortion which went wrong and they went off to the South of France to recuperate. And there, apparently, had an idyllic time.

This idyll had continued up until the previous Saturday, 1st December, when they last met. That was the day after the Sally Nash trial started, and the day that Marius

Steen's terrible show, *Sex of One and Half a Dozen of the Other*, celebrated a thousand performances. And from that day on Jacqui had been unable to contact Steen. He had very deliberately told her to get lost, and when she didn't take the hint, he'd sent her an obscene note. And according to Jacqui, the reason for this must be Steen's fear of her being associated with him in the Sally Nash case because it might affect his chances of a knighthood. It was preposterous. Nobody would behave like that.

Charles wasn't sure whether Jacqui believed she was telling the truth or not. She might have her own reasons for obscuring the issue. But, leaving that aside for a moment, he tried to make some sense of Steen's behaviour.

The simplest explanation was that he had just got tired of Jacqui. That was quite possible, however well she thought the affair was going. He was a man who had always put it about a bit, as Harry Chiltern said. Jacqui was an attractive enough bit of stuff, but there were hundreds more like her and why should he stick to one? He'd be very unlikely to stay with her or marry her, particularly with a knighthood in the offing. As Jacqui herself admitted, she wasn't the sort of consort for a 'do with the Queen Mum.'

And, Charles's mind raced on, Steen could have picked up a new tottie at the *Sex for One . . .* party on the Saturday night. That would explain the sudden change in his affections.

But as he thought of it, Charles knew the explanation was inadequate. Even if that had happened, it didn't justify the violence of Steen's attempts to get Jacqui off his back.

No, Steen's behaviour certainly suggested that he regarded her as a threat in some way. Perhaps she had tried to blackmail him . . . ? Yes, that made sense. She had actually tried to use the photographs . . . perhaps to blackmail him into marrying her. (That would tie in with the pregnancy in the summer—an earlier attempt to force Steen's hand.) She could have tried the blackmail approach on the Saturday afternoon; then, when Steen cut up rough, she realised she'd over-stepped the mark and brought in Charles as a go-between to patch things up. That would even explain why she took him back to Archer Street from the Montrose. She'd just gone down there to look for any good-natured sucker.

But the new explanation wasn't much more satisfactory than the first. For a start, Charles didn't like to think of Jacqui in that light. And also he doubted whether she had the intelligence to be so devious. The only convincing bit was the thought of Steen as a frightened man. What was it he was afraid of?

Charles marshalled his knowledge of blackmailers' habits. It was limited, all gleaned from detective novels. He got out the brown envelope and spread the photographs on his lap. His reaction to them had numbed. They just seemed slightly unwholesome now, like used tissues. Just photographs. What would Sherlock Holmes, Lord Peter Wimsey, Hercule Poirot and the rest have made of that lot? Charles made a cursory check for blood-stained fingerprints, the thread of a sports jacket made from tweed only available in a small tailor's shop in Aberdeen, the scratch marks of an artificial hand or the faint but unmistakeable aroma of orange blossom. The investigation, he concluded without surprise, yielded negative results. They were just photographs.

Just photographs. The phrase caught in his mind. Negative results. Yes, of course. Where were the bloody negatives? Jacqui had paid out a thousand pounds for something that could be reproduced at will. A very rudimentary knowledge of detective fiction tells you that any photographic blackmailer worth his salt keeps producing copies of the incriminating material until he's blue in the face. It would be typical of Jacqui's naïveté to believe that she was dealing with an honest man who had given her the only copies in existence.

If this were so, and the photographer was putting pressure on him, then Steen's reactions were consistent. He had reason to be frightened. But why should he be frightened of Jacqui? Charles shuffled through his pockets for a two p piece and went down to the phone.

'Jacqui?'

'Yes.' She sounded very low.

'All right?'

'Not too good.'

'Listen, Jacqui, I think I may be on to something about the way Steen's behaving.'

'What?' She sounded perkier instantly.

'Jacqui, you've got to tell me the truth. When you bought those photographs . . .'

'Yes?'

'Did you buy the negatives, too?'

'No. I didn't. But he'd destroyed them. He said so.'

'I see. And did you mention to Steen that you'd got the photographs at any time?'

'No. I wanted it to be a surprise—a present. He had mentioned them vaguely, said he was a bit worried. So I fixed to get them.'

'When were they actually handed over to you?'

'Last Saturday evening.'

'And you never mentioned them even when you tried to ring Steen?'

'I started to. On the Sunday evening when I first rang him. I spoke to Nigel. I said it was about the photographs, but even before I'd finished talking, he gave me this message from Marius to . . . you know . . . to get lost.'

'Right. Give me the name and address of the bloke you got the photos from.'

As Charles limped along Praed Street, he began to regret dressing up for the encounter, but when he reflected on the exceptional violence of blackmailers in all detective fiction, he decided it was as well to conceal his identity. The disguise was good and added ten years to him. He'd grayed his temples and eyebrows with a spray, and parted his hair on the other side. He was wearing the démodé pin-striped suit he'd got from a junk-shop for a production of *Arturo Ui* ('grossly over-played'—*Glasgow Herald*) and the tie he'd worn as Harry in *Marching Song* ('adequate if uninspiring'—*Oxford Mail*). He walked with the limp he'd used in *Richard III* ('nicely understated'—*Yorkshire Post*). He wasn't sure whether to speak in the accent he'd used in *Look Back in Anger* ('a splendid Blimp'—*Worcester Gazette*) or the one for *When We Are Married* ('made a meal of the part'—*Croydon Advertiser*).

'Imago Studios,' the address Jacqui had given him, proved to be in a tatty mews near St Mary's Hospital in Paddington. The downstairs stable-garage part had apparently been converted into a studio. On the windows of the upper part the curtains were drawn. Charles rang the bell. Nothing. He rang again and heard movement.

The door was opened by a woman in a pale pink nylon housecoat and pink fur slippers. She had prominent teeth and dyed black hair swept back in the style of a souvenir Greek goddess. Her face was heavily made up and eyelashed. Charles couldn't help thinking of a hard pink meringue full of artificial cream.

She looked at him hard. 'Yes?'

'Ah, good afternoon.' Charles plumped for the *When We Are Married* accent. 'I wondered if Bill was in.'

Jacqui had only given him the Christian name. It was all she knew.

'Who are you? What do you want with him?'

'My name's Holroyd. Bill Holroyd.' On the spur of the moment he couldn't think of another Christian name. He grinned weakly. 'Both called Bill, eh?'

'What's it about?'

'Some photographs.'

'What is it—wedding or portrait? Because my husband—'

'No, no, it's a more . . . personal sort of thing.'

'Ah.' She knew what he meant. 'You better come in.'

She led the way up the very steep stairs. The large nylon-clad bottom swished close to Charles's face as he limped up after her. 'Can you manage?'

'Yes. It's just my gammy leg.'

'How did you do it, Mr Holroyd?'

'In the war.'

'Jumping out of some tart's bedroom window, I suppose. That's where most war wounds came from.'

'No. Mine was a genuine piece of shrapnel.'

'Huh.' She ushered him into a stuffy little room lit by bright spotlights. It was decorated in orange and yellow, with a leopardette three-piece suite covering most of the carpet. Every available surface was crowded with small brass souvenirs. Lincoln imps, windjammer bells, lighthouses, anchor thermometers, knights in armour, wishing wells, everything. On the dresser two posed and tinted photographs rose from the undergrowth of brass. One was the woman, younger, but still with her Grecian hair and heavy make-up. The other was of a man, plumpish and vaguely familiar.

The woman pointed to an armchair. 'Sit down. Rest your shrapnel.'

'Thank you.'

She slumped back on to the sofa, revealing quite a lot

of bare thigh. 'Right, Mr Holroyd, what's it about?'

'I was hoping to see your husband.'

'He's . . . er . . . he's not here at the moment, but I know about the business.'

'I see. When are you expecting him back?'

'You can deal with me,' she said. Hard.

'Right, Mrs . . . er?'

'Sweet.'

'Mrs Sweet.' Charles was tempted to make a quaint Yorkshire pleasantry about the name, but looked at Mrs Sweet and decided against it. 'This is, you understand, a rather delicate matter . . .'

'I understand.'

'It's . . . er . . . the fact is . . . Last summer I was down in London on business and . . . er . . . it happened that, by chance . . . through some friends, I ended up at a party given by . . . er . . . well, some people in Holland Park. Near Holland Park, that is . . .'

'Yes.' She didn't give anything.'

'Yes . . . Yes . . . Well, I believe that . . . er . . . your husband was at this particular party . . .'

'Maybe.'

'In fact, I believe he took some photographs at the party.'

'Look here, are you from the police? I've had enough of them round this week.'

'What?' Charles blustered and looked affronted for a moment while he took this in. Obviously the police had been making enquiries about the Sally Nash case. Marius Steen's anxiety was justified. 'No, of course I'm not from the police. I'm the director of a man-made fibres company,' he said, with a flash of inspiration.

'Thank God. I couldn't take any more of that lot.'

'No, no. The fact is, Mrs Sweet, that . . . er . . . I am, you see, a married man. I have two lovely daughters at boarding school and . . . er . . . well, I have become rather anxious about these . . . er . . . photographs.'

'Yes.' She didn't volunteer anything.

'I have come to the right place, have I? I mean, your husband was at this party in . . . ?'

'Yes. He was there.' She paused and looked at him, assessing. 'Well, Mr Holroyd, I think I know which photographs you are referring to. Of course, photography's an expensive business.'

'I understand that, Mrs Sweet. How much do you think your husband would part with the . . . er . . . photographs for?'

'Two thousand pounds.'

'That's a lot of money.' The price has gone up, thought Charles. 'And would that be for the negatives as well?'

'Ah, Mr Holroyd. How shrewd you are. No, I'm afraid not. The photographs *and* the negatives would cost you five thousand pounds.'

So, as he suspected, Jacqui had been done. A thousand pounds for one set of photographs; there might be any number of others about. Bill Holroyd blustered. 'Oh, I don't think I could possibly raise that.'

'That's the price. Mind you, when things start moving in a certain court case, they might get even more expensive.'

'Oh, dear.' Charles let a note of panic creep into Bill Holroyd's voice and looked anxiously around the room.

'No point in looking for them, love.' It was 'love,' now she knew she had the whip hand. 'You won't find them here.'

'How do I know you've got them?'

'I'll show you.' She opened a drawer in the dresser, pulled out a folder and handed it to him. 'Only copies, love. You'll never find the negatives, so don't try.'

'No.' Charles opened the folder and looked at all the photographs. There were a lot and they included some identical to the set still bulging in his pocket. His hunch about the morals of blackmailing photographers was right. He handed them back. 'You don't think there's any possibility that the price might be—'

'Five thousand pounds.'

'Hmm.' (A pause, while Charles tried, according to the best Stanislavskian method, to give the impression of a man torn between the two great motives of his life—love of money and fear of scandal.) 'Of course, it would take me some time to put my hands on that amount of money. Some days.'

'I can wait.' She smiled like a Venus fly-trap. 'I'm not so sure that you can. Once they start getting deeper into this trial, I'm sure the interest in photographs of this sort will—'

'Yes, yes. I'm sure it won't take too long. It's unfortunate not having my bank in London. It's in Leeds. But . . . er . . . perhaps by Wednesday . . . Would Wednesday . . . ?'

'I'll be here. With the negatives.'

'Oh good.' Although he was only acting the part, Charles felt Bill Holroyd's relief. And in his own character he'd found out what he wanted to know. If there were other copies of the photographs, there was no doubt that Bill Sweet was blackmailing Steen. Steen had assumed from Jacqui's message to Nigel that she was involved too. Charles was relieved that the information put her in the clear; she had been telling the truth. All he had to do now was what she had asked—get to see Steen, give him the photographs and explain that Jacqui was nothing to do with Bill Sweet. If Sweet himself continued his blackmail, that wasn't Charles's concern.

Mrs Sweet rose from the sofa. 'That's our business concluded. I'm glad we reached agreement in such a reasonable way. Would you like a drink?'

'Oh, thank you very much.' Perhaps a little too readily

for Bill Holroyd. 'That is to say, I don't make a habit of it, but perhaps a small one.'

'Gin?' She went to the door.

'That'd be . . . very nice.' Charles just stopped himself from saying 'Reet nice.' Would have been too much.

After a few moments, Mrs Sweet returned with a bottle, poured two substantial gins, added tonic and proffered a glass. Charles rose to take it. They were close. She didn't move back. 'Cheers, Mr Holroyd.'

'Cheers.'

She looked at him, hard. 'You like all that, do you, Mr Holroyd?'

'All what?'

'Parties. Like the one in Holland Park.'

'Oh . . . well. Not habitually, no. I'm a respectable man, but, you know, one works very hard and . . . er . . . needs to relax, eh?'

'Yes.' She sat back on the sofa and motioned him beside her. 'Yes, I find I need to relax too, Mr Holroyd.'

'Ah.' Charles sat gingerly on the mock leopard. He couldn't quite believe the way things appeared to be going, and couldn't think of anything else to say.

But Mrs Sweet continued, softly. 'Yes, and relaxation becomes increasingly difficult.' Her hand rested gently on top of his. The scene was getting distinctly sultry.

Charles decided to play it for light comedy. 'I go in for a certain amount of golf, you know. That's good for relaxation.'

'Oh, really.' Her hand was moving gently over his. Charles stole a sidelong glance. The mouth was parted and thickened lashes low over her eyes. He recognised that she was trying to look seductive, and, while he didn't find her attractive (rather the reverse), he was intrigued by the sudden change in her behaviour.

Mrs Sweet leaned against him, so that he could feel the lacquered crispness of her hair on his ear. Her hand drew his to rest casually on her thigh. 'I've never played golf.'

'Oh, it's a grand game,' said Charles fatuously. In spite of himself, he could feel that he was becoming interested. Her perfume was strong and acrid in his nostrils. 'Champion game.'

'But I'm sure you play others.' Quite suddenly the grip hardened on his hand and he felt it forced into the warm cleft between her legs. Instinctively he clutched at the nylon-clad mound.

But his mind was moving quickly. Mrs Sweet and her husband were blackmailers. This must be a plot of some sort. 'Where's your husband?'

'A long way away.'

'But wouldn't he mind if—'

'We lead separate lives. Very separate lives now.' Her face was close to his and he kissed her. After all, he reflected, I am one of the few people in the world who isn't worth blackmailing. And Bill Holroyd was already showing himself to be pretty gullible, so it's in character.

Mrs Sweet reached her free hand down to his flies. No impotence problem this time. Charles began to consider the irony of life—that with Jacqui, whom he found very attractive, there was nothing, and yet with this nymphomaniac, who almost repelled him . . . but it wasn't the moment for philosophy.

Mrs Sweet stood up and stripped off the housecoat. There was a crackle of static electricity. Her underwear was lacy red and black, brief and garish, the kind of stuff he'd seen in Soho shops and assumed was the monopoly of prostitutes. Perhaps she was a prostitute. The thought of another dose of clap flashed across his mind. But he was by now too aroused to be side-tracked.

He hastily pulled off his clothes and stood facing Mrs Sweet.

'It doesn't show,' she said.

'What?'

'Your war wound. The shrapnel.'

'Ah. No. Well, they do wonders with plastic surgery.' He advanced and put his arms round her, fumbled with the back of her brassiere. 'The front,' she murmured. It unclipped.

They sank down on to the leopardette sofa and he slipped off the crisp lacy briefs. Underneath he'd expected her to be hard and dry, but she was very soft and moist. Again he thought of meringues. And as he had her, he emitted grunts which he hoped were in character for the director of a man-made fibres company.

CHAPTER SEVEN

CINDERELLA BY THE FIRESIDE

Charles felt distinctly jaded as he walked along Hereford Road. Mrs Sweet had kept him at it some time. He ached all over, and felt the revulsion that sex without affection always left like a hangover inside him. It was half-past four and dark. No pubs open yet. He felt in need of a bath to wash away Mrs Sweet's stale perfume.

As he entered the hall of the house, he heard a door open upstairs. 'He is here,' said a flat Swedish voice. There was the sound of footsteps running downstairs and Jacqui rushed into his arms. She was quivering like an animal. He held her to him and she started to weep hysterically. A podgy Swedish face peered over the banisters at them. 'You are an old dirty man,' it said and disappeared.

Charles was too concerned with Jacqui even to yell the usual obscenities at the Swede. He led the trembling girl into his room. She was as cold as ice. He sat her in the armchair and lit the gas-fire, poured a large Scotch and held it out to her. 'No. It'd make me sick.' And she burst out crying again.

Charles knelt by the chair and put his arm round her shoulders. She was still shivering convulsively. 'What's happened, Jacqui?'

The question prompted another great surge of weeping. Charles stayed crouching by her side and drank the Scotch while he tried to think how to calm her.

Eventually the convulsions subsided to some extent and he could hear what she was saying. 'My flat—they broke into my flat.'

'Who did?'

'I don't know. This morning I came back from doing the weekend shopping and it was—it had all been done over. My oil lamp—and the curtains pulled down and all my glasses smashed and my clothes torn in shreds and—' She broke down again into incoherence.

'Jacqui, who did it?'

'I don't know. It must have been someone who Marius—who Marius—' she sobbed.

'Why should he—'

'I . . . I tried to ring him again.'

'Jacqui, I told you not to do that.'

'I know, but I . . . I couldn't help it . . . I had to ring him, because of the baby.'

'Baby?'

'Yes, I'm pregnant again and . . .'

'Does Steen know?'

'Yes. We knew a month ago, and he said we'd keep this one and he wanted a child and . . .' Again she was shaken by uncontrollable spasms.

'Jacqui, listen. Calm down. Listen, it'll be all right. Steen's only acting this way because he's frightened. There's been a misunderstanding about those photographs.' And Charles gave an edited version of his findings at Imago Studios.

By the end of his narrative she was calmer. 'So that's all. Marius thinks I'm involved with this Bill Sweet?'

'That's it. Jacqui, you might have known he'd keep the negatives.'

'I never thought. I hope you tore him off a strip when—'

'I didn't see him. I saw his wife.'

'What was she like?'

'Oh.' He shrugged non-committally. 'Listen, Jacqui, it'll be all right now. You can stay here. You'll be quite safe. And go ahead as planned. I'll somehow get to see Steen, deliver the photographs and explain the position.

Then at least he'll take the heat off you. And turn it on Sweet, where it belongs.' He laughed. 'I must say, Jacqui, I don't care for your boyfriend's methods.'

Jacqui laughed too, a weak giggle of relief. 'Yes, he can be a bastard. You think it'll be all right?'

'Just as soon as I can get to see him. I mean, I don't know about the emotional thing—that's between the two of you—but I'm sure he'll stop the rough stuff.'

There was a pause. Jacqui breathed deeply. 'Oh, it really hurts. My throat, from all that crying.'

'Yes, of course it does. You're exhausted. Tell you what, I'll get you pleasantly drunk, tuck you up in bed, you'll sleep the sleep of the dead. And in the morning nothing'll seem so bad.'

'But my flat . . .'

'I'll help you tidy it up, when we've got this sorted out.'

'Oh, Charles, you are great. I don't know what I'd do without you, honest.'

''S'all right.' He took her hand and gripped it, embarrassed, like a father with his grown-up daughter. Then suddenly, brisk. 'Right, I'm hungry. Have you had anything to eat?'

'No, I . . . I've felt sick. I—'

'Haven't got anything here, but—'

'I couldn't go out.'

'Don't you worry. It was for just such occasions that fish and chips were invented.'

'Oh, no. I'd be sick.'

'Don't you believe it. Nice bit of rock salmon, bag of chips, lots of vinegar, you'll feel on top of the world.'

'Ugh.'

It's strange how fish and chip newspapers, out of date and greasy, are always much more interesting than current ones. It's like other people's papers in crowded tubes. You can't wait to buy a copy and read some intriguing article you glimpse over a strap-hanging shoulder. It's always disappointing.

In the fish and chip shop Charles noticed that his order was wrapped in a copy of the *Sun*. On the front page was the tantalising headline, 'Virginity Auction—see page 11.' The fascination of page 11 grew as he walked home. Who was auctioning whose virginity to whom? And where?

This thought preoccupied him as he entered his room. Jacqui was lying on the bed, fast asleep. Curled up in a ball on the candlewick, she looked about three years old.

He made no attempt to wake her. In her state sleep was more important than food. The Virginity Auction—he settled down in front of the fire to find out all about it. He slipped a hot crumbling piece of fish into his mouth, placed the warm bag of chips on his knees and turned to page 11.

Bugger. He'd only got pages 1 to 8, and the corresponding ones at the back. He'd never know where virginities were knocked down, or how one bidded. A pleasant thought of nubile young girls being displayed at Sotheby's crossed his mind.

There wasn't much else in the paper. It was the last Wednesday's—all bloody petrol crisis. The titty girl on page 3's midriff was stained and transparent with grease from the fish and chips. It looked rather obscene, particularly as the word 'Come' showed through backwards from the other side of the page.

Charles turned over and stopped dead. There was a photograph on the page that was ominously familiar. He had last seen it on a dresser, surrounded by brass souvenirs.

Fiercely calm, he read the accompanying article.

M4 MURDER VICTIM IDENTIFIED

The man whose body was found early on Monday morning by the M4 exit road at Theale, Berks, has been identified as 44-year-old William Sweet, a photographer from Paddington, London. Sweet was found shot through the head at the roadside beside his grey Ford Escort, which appeared to have run out of petrol.

Interviewed at his Paddington studios, Sweet's wife, Audrey, could suggest no motive for the killing. Police believe Sweet may have been the victim of a gangland revenge killing, and that he may have been mistaken for someone else.

Charles put down the fish and chips and poured a large Scotch. He could feel his thoughts beginning to stampede and furiously tried to hold them in check.

Certain points were clear. He ordered them with grim concentration. Marius Steen must have killed Sweet: Sweet had put the pressure on about the photographs, Steen had fixed to meet him and shot him. Charles grabbed an old AA book that was lying around. Yes, the Theale turn-off was the one you'd take going to Streatley. Sweet was shot Sunday night or Monday morning. Marius Steen was in London certainly on the Saturday night, because he was at the *Sex of One . . .* party. And in Streatley during the week. He was therefore likely to have been driving through Theale late on Sunday. As Harry Chiltern had said, there was always a gun in the glove compartment. A glance at the map made Charles pretty sure that that gun was now in the Thames.

Other facts followed too. Mrs Sweet was holding out on the police. It was nonsense for her to say no one had a motive for murdering her husband. As Charles had discovered, she knew about the Sally Nash party photographs. All she had to do was to tell the police about her husband's blackmailing activities and very soon the finger would point at Steen. For reasons of her own, she wasn't doing that. Probably just didn't want to lose a profitable business.

But the most chilling deduction from the fact of Bill Sweet's murder was the immediate danger to Jacqui. If he'd shoot one person who challenged him, Marius Steen would do the same to anyone else he thought represented the same threat. He'd tried to frighten Jacqui off with the telephone messages and vicious note, but if she persisted . . . Charles shivered as he thought what might have happened if Jacqui had been in the flat when her 'visitors' called that morning. He looked over to the child-like form on his bed and felt a protective instinct so strong he almost wept.

Confrontation with Marius Steen couldn't wait. Charles must get down to Streatley straight away. If the man was down there . . . Better ring the Bayswater house to check. But he hadn't got the number. It seemed a pity to wake Jacqui. He opened her handbag, but the address book revealed nothing.

No help for it. 'Jacqui.' He shook her gently. She started like a frightened cat, and looked up at him wide-eyed. 'Sorry. Listen, I've been thinking. I want to get this sorted out, like as soon as possible. There's no point in your being in this state of terror. I am going to try and see Steen tonight. Get it over with.'

'But if he's in Streatley—'

'That's all right. I don't mind.' He tried to sound casual, as if the new urgency was only a whim. 'My daughter lives down that way. I wanted to go and visit her anyway.'

'I didn't know you'd got a daughter.'

'Oh, yes.'

'How old?'

'Twenty-one.'

'Nearly as old as me.'

'Yes.'

'Like me?'

'Hardly. Safely married at nineteen to a whizz-kid of the insurance world—if that's not a contradiction in terms. Anyway, the reason I woke you was not just bloody-mindedness. I want to ring Steen's Bayswater place and check he's not there. It's a long way to go if he's just round the corner.'

Both the phone numbers Jacqui gave were ex-directory. Charles paused for a moment before dialling the Bayswater one, while he decided what character to take on. It had to be someone anonymous, but somebody who would be allowed to speak to the man if he was there, and someone who might conceivably be ringing on a Saturday night.

The phone was picked up at the other end and Charles pressed his two p into the coinbox. A discreet, educated voice identified the number—nothing more.

'Ah, good evening.' He plumped for the Glaswegian accent he'd used in a Thirty-Minute Theatre ('Pointless'—*The Times*). 'Is that Mr Marius Steen's residence?'

'He does live here, yes, but—'

'It's Detective-Sergeant McWhirter from Scotland Yard. I'm sorry to bother you at this time of night. Is it possible to speak to Mr Steen?'

'I'm afraid not. Mr Steen is at his home in the country. Can I help at all?'

Charles hadn't planned beyond finding out what he wanted to know and had to think quickly. 'Ah yes, perhaps you can. It's only a small thing. Um.' Playing for time. Then a sudden flash of inspiration. 'We're just checking on various Rolls-Royce owners. There's a number-plate racket going on at the moment. I wonder if you could give me Mr Steen's registration.'

The discreet voice did so. 'Thank you very much. That's all I wanted to know. I'm so sorry to have troubled you. Goodbye.'

As Charles put the phone down, he tried to work out what on earth a number-plate racket might be. It was quite meaningless, but at least he'd got the required information.

He tried the Berkshire number. The phone rang for about thirty seconds, then after a click, a voice gave the number and said, 'This is Marius Steen speaking on one of these recorded answering contraptions. I am either out at the moment or busy working on some scripts and don't want to talk right now. If your message is business ring the office—' he gave the number '—on Monday, if it's really urgent, you can leave a message on this machine, and if you want money, get lost.' A pause. 'Hello. Are you still there? Right then, after this whiney noise, tell me what it is.' Then the tone, then silence.

The voice was striking. Charles felt he must have heard Steen being interviewed at some stage on radio or television, because it was very familiar. And distinctive. The Polish origins had been almost eroded, but not quite; they had been overlaid with heavy Cockney, which, in turn, had been flattened into a classier accent as Steen climbed the social ladder. As an actor, Charles could feel all the elements in the voice and begin to feel something of the man. He dialled the number again just to hear the voice and find out what else it could tell him.

The message itself was odd. The first reaction to 'if you want money, get lost' was that Steen must be referring to potential blackmailers, but then Charles realised how unlikely that was. Any of Steen's friends might ring him, so the message had to have a more general application. Most likely it was just a joke. After all, Steen was notorious for his success with money. And notoriously tight-fisted. Tight as a bottle-top, as Harry Chiltern had said. For him to make that sort of joke on the recording was in keeping with the impression Charles was beginning to form of his character.

And in spite of everything, that impression was good. Somehow Steen's voice seemed to confirm Jacqui's view. It was rich with character and humour. The whole tone of the recording was of a man who was alive in the sense that mattered, the sort of man Charles felt he would like when he met him. And yet this was also the man who had recently shot a blackmailer through the head.

Somehow even that seemed suddenly consistent. A man as big as Steen shouldn't have to be involved with little second-rate crooks like Bill Sweet. Charles felt more hopeful about his mission, certain that when he actually got to Steen, he'd be able to talk to him and clear Jacqui from his suspicions.

He tried Juliet and Miles's phone number in Pangbourne, but there was no reply. No doubt out for the evening talking insurance at some scampi supper. Marius Steen might be out too, but he was bound to return at some stage, and the more Charles thought about the urgency of the situation, the more he was determined to meet the man.

He said goodbye to Jacqui. She refused the cold remains of the fish and chips, so he took the whole package out to the dustbin at the front of the house (no need to worry her about the Sweet murder it she didn't know—and it appeared she didn't). He caught a train from Paddington to Reading, arrived there to find the last train to Goring and Streatley had gone, and, after a considerable wait, got a minicab.

It was only when he was sitting in the back of the car that he actually thought of the risk he was taking. Because of a mild affection for a tart he now seemed unable even to make love to, he was going to confront a man he knew to be a murderer with copies of the photographs for which a man had been killed. Put like that, it did sound rather silly. Fortunately, there had been time to buy a half bottle of Bell's on the way to Paddington. Charles took a long pull. And another one.

The car drew up outside a pair of high white gates. The driver charged an enormous amount of money 'on account of the petrol crisis' and swore when he wasn't given a tip to match. As the car's lights disappeared round the corner, it occurred to Charles that he should perhaps have asked the man to wait. If Steen turned nasty, he'd be glad of a quick getaway. But the thought was too late.

It was now very cold, the night air sharp and clear. The moon was nearly full and shed a watery light on the scene. It gleamed dully from a puddle outside the gates, which were high and solid, made of interlocking vertical planks. A fluorescent bell-push shone on the stone post to the right. Charles pressed it for a long time. It was now after midnight. Steen might well be in bed.

He pressed the button at intervals for about five minutes, but there was no reaction. His quarry might not be back yet, or perhaps the bell wasn't working. Charles tried the latch of the gate; he had to push hard but eventually it yielded.

He stood on a gravel path, looking at the house. It was an enormous bungalow, with a central block roofed in green tiles which shone in the moonlight. From this main part smaller wings spread off like the suburbs of a city. To the right there was a ramp down to a double garage on basement level. The whole building was painted the frost white of cake icing and its shine echoed the gleam of the silent Thames behind. No lights showed.

The main door was sheltered by a portico with tall columns, an incongruous touch of Ancient Greece grafted on to the sprawling modern bungalow. The door itself was of dark panelled wood with a brass knocker. Since there was no sign of a bell, Charles raised the enormous ring and let it fall.

The noise shocked him. It boomed as if the whole house was a resonating chamber for the brass instrument on the door. Charles waited, then knocked again. Soon he was hammering on the door, thud after thud, a noise fit to wake the dead. But there was nothing. The rush to Berkshire had been pointless. The photographs still bulged in his inside pocket. Marius Steen was not at home.

CHAPTER EIGHT

INSIDE THE GIANT'S CASTLE

'It would have all been easier, Daddy,' said Juliet, 'if you'd had some sort of regular job. I mean, acting's so unpredictable.'

'No, no, darling,' said Miles Taylerson, judiciously, 'not all acting. I mean there are regular jobs in acting—you know, directors of repertory companies, or in serials like *Coronation Street* or *Crossroads*.'

Charles, seated in Miles's karate-style dressing gown, gritted his teeth and buttered, or rather battered, a piece of toast.

'No, but, quite honestly, Daddy, I do worry about you. I mean, you haven't set anything aside for your old age.'

'This is my old age, so it's too late now,' Charles pronounced with facetious finality.

But unfortunately that was not a conversation-stopper for Miles; it was a cue. 'Oh, I wouldn't say that, Pop'—Charles winced—'I mean, there are insurance plans and pension plans for people of any age. In fact, in my company we have rather a good scheme. I know of a fellow of over sixty who took out a policy. Of course, the premiums are high, but it's linked to a unit trust, so it's with profits.'

'I thought unit trusts were doing rather badly,' Charles tried maliciously, but Miles was unruffled.

'Oh yes, there haven't been the spectacular rises of the first few years, but we could guarantee a growth figure which more than copes with inflation. I know a case of a fellow who—'

Charles couldn't stand the prospect of another textbook example. 'Miles, I didn't come down here to talk about insurance.'

'Sorry, Pop. It's only because we're concerned about you. Isn't that so, darling?'

'Yes. You see, Daddy, Miles and I do worry. You don't seem to have any sense of direction since you left Mummy. We'd just feel happier if we'd thought you'd made some provisions for the future.'

'Exactly, darling. And, Pop, now you've got the advantage of someone in insurance actually in the family, it makes it so much easier.'

'What? You mean it's easier than having some creep loaded with policies pestering me at my digs—'

'Yes.'

'—to have a creep in the family doing exactly the same thing.'

A pause ensued. Miles went very red, muttered something about 'things to get on with' and left the room. Charles munched his toast.

'Daddy, there's no need to be rude to Miles.'

'I'm sorry, but it is tempting.'

'Look, he's been jolly tolerant. You arriving completely unannounced in the middle of the night, using our house as a hotel. We might have had people staying. As it is, he's put off his fishing so as to entertain you—'

'That was entertainment? My God, what's he like when he's not making an effort?'

Juliet ignored him. 'And I think you might show a bit of gratitude. Daddy, I do wish you'd just get yourself sorted out.'

Oh, sharper than the serpent's tooth it is, to have an ungrateful father. But, Charles reflected, ever sharper to have a middle-aged daughter of twenty-one. Where had he gone wrong, as a parent? There must have been a moment when Juliet had shown some spark of individuality which he failed to foster. Some moment when she, as a child, was on the verge of doing something wrong, and he could have fulfilled a father's role and made her do it. But no, his daughter had always been a model of sobriety, good works and even chastity. A virgin when she married at nineteen. In 1973. So much for the permissive society. It's disappointing for a father.

Miles reappeared, incongruously dressed in brand-new green waders, a brand-new camouflage jacket and brand-new shapeless hat. 'Look, Pop, sorry we got heated.'

'No one got heated. I was just rather rude to you.'

Miles laughed in man-of-the-world style. 'Jolly good, Pop. That's what I like. Straight talking. Eh? Look, what I wondered was, would you like to come fishing with me? Got time for a couple of hours, then a quick pint at the local, while Juliet gets the lunch. What do you say?'

'Well, I should be—' Charles remembered his mission.

'We could go into Streatley, there's a nice pub there.'

'Oh, all right.' It was important to get there and a lift in Miles's odious yellow Cortina was as good a way as any other. He graciously accepted the olive branch.

Charles persuaded a rather grudging Miles that he had time for a quick bath before they left. It was still only half-past nine. Apparently it was Miles's fishing that got them up so early. Charles wondered. To him, getting up early on a Sunday seemed sacrilegious, particularly if you had a woman around. Some of the best times of his life had been Sunday mornings. Toast, newspapers and a warm body. Not for the first time, he tried to visualise his daughter's sex-life. It defied imagination. Perhaps a regular weekly deposit with a family protective policy and a bonus of an extra screw at age twenty-five.

As he lay in the marine blue bath (matching the marine blue wash-basin and separate lavatory), laced with Juliet's bubble bath, Charles thought about the Steen situation. It seemed a long way away and he focused his mind with an effort. Assuming he could see Steen and hand over the photographs, it would soon be over. Now Bill Sweet was dead, there was no one else to put on the pressure. Charles conveniently put the circumstances of Sweet's death to the back of his mind. He didn't feel any obligation to see justice done in that matter. If Steen was a murderer, that wasn't his business. Let the police deal with it. If they really wanted to find a motive for the murder, they should grill Mrs Sweet. She could supply them with a few answers.

But did Mrs Sweet know about Steen? Had she realised who was responsible for her husband's death? In fact, did she know all the details of his blackmailing activities or was she just cashing in as much as possible? If Mrs Sweet was in the picture, she might continue the pressure on Steen, and that could have unpleasant repercussions for Jacqui. It suddenly became rather urgent to find out how much Mrs Sweet knew.

The trouble with modern architect-designed houses on estates (what's the alternative to an architect-designed house—a milkman-designed house? a footballer-designed house?) is that there's no privacy. The telephone in the Taylersons' executive home was situated in the middle of the open-plan living area, which had unimpeded access to the kitchen area, the sitting area and the upstairs area. In other words, Juliet and Miles were bound to hear every word of any telephone conversation. But there was no alternative.

The ringing tone stopped. 'Hello.'

'Ah, Mrs Sweet. It's . . . er . . . Bill Holroyd.' The old *When We Are Married* voice.

'Ah, Mr Holroyd.' Interest.

'Yes . . . er, the reason I'm ringing is . . . er . . . I've just heard about your husband . . .'

'Yes.' No emotion.

'I wondered if . . . er . . . this changed the situation?'

'No. You deal with me.'

'Yes. Er . . . nasty business.' No reaction. 'This doesn't mean that the . . . er . . . police . . . would . . . er . . .'

'Don't worry. I haven't told them a thing.'

'Oh, good.'

'Yes. You just give me what you owe and you'll never hear about that particular business again.'

'Fine. There was . . . er . . . something else. One or two of my friends were also at the party . . .'

'Yes.'

'A Mr Phillips, a Mr Cuthbertson, a Mr—' he tried desperately to think of a name '—Taylerson. They . . . er . . . wondered if they featured in the photographs.'

'Yes, I rather think they did. You'd better put them in touch with me.'

'Yes.' Charles was getting the information he wanted. Obviously Mrs Sweet hadn't a clue who any of the people in the photographs were. But best to be sure. 'Mr Taylerson in particular was anxious. He seemed to think he might feature in some pictures with a blonde girl. And a mask.' The Steen and Jacqui photographs were the only ones that fitted the description.

'That's Mr Taylerson, ah.' She didn't know. 'Perhaps I'd better get in touch with him. Do you know his address?'

Charles resisted the temptation to give Miles's address, funny though the image of his son-in-law being blackmailed with dirty photographs was. 'No, I think I'd better put him in touch with you.'

'Yes, do that. And I'll see you Wednesday.'

'Yes.'

'With the money.'

'Yes.'

'And . . .' the voice continued with studied casualness, 'perhaps you'd better double the money . . .'

'What?'

'Mr Holroyd, you remember yesterday afternoon?'

'Yes.'

'Well, would you believe it, Mr Holroyd, there's a camera trained on that sofa.'

'Oh.'

'I'm sure you wouldn't want your wife and two lovely daughters to—'

'No.'

'Ten thousand then, Mr Holroyd, and you'll have the whole album.'

'But I—' The line went dead. Charles felt enormous relief that he wasn't Bill Holroyd. Bill Holroyd was a man with problems. Still, it explained Mrs Sweet's sudden change of behaviour. Oh dear, and he'd thought it was his own animal magnetism.

Charles turned to see Miles and Juliet standing open-mouthed in the kitchen doorway. 'Sorry about that. Talking to an actress friend. Always fool about like that. Putting on voices.'

'Yes,' said Miles in a very old-fashioned voice. 'I suppose a lot of that sort of thing goes on with actors and . . . you know. Perhaps we can go fishing now.'

'Just one more call. Will be quick, I promise. What's the code for Streatley from here?'

Again it was a recorded answer. Steen's voice gave the number. 'Marius Steen speaking. Not available at the moment. Ring later, or leave a message after this noise.'

Miles had the complete kit. Not only the shining new camouflage clothes, but various shining new containers of tackle. A waterproof khaki bag to hang from one shoulder, a long black leather rod-case to hang from the other, and an assortment of neatly dangling nets, stools and bait-boxes. As he laid out his instruments on squares of cloth like a surgeon, he said, 'You know, Pop, fishing's a very good relaxant. Relaxation is important to anyone in an executive position.'

They were sitting on the bank opposite Steen's house, Miles on a new folding chair of shining chromium tubes, Charles on a relegated wooden stool. He had chosen the location deliberately, assuring Miles that it was a very promising swim, that the swirlings of the current denoted barbel pits and that the overhanging trees were a good lie for large pike. It was all nonsense, but it was in the right language and Miles was impressed.

So Charles had a good view. The bungalow didn't look so large from the back, just discreetly expensive, a low white outline from which the lawn sloped gently down to a neat concreted waterside. To the left there was a small boat-house whose locked doors gave on to the river.

The bungalow showed no sign of life, and there had not been any when they had driven past on the road. Charles had persuaded Miles to stop and tried ringing the bell on the gate. No reply.

But somebody had been there overnight. Not only was there the evidence of the changed recording on the telephone. The puddles outside the bungalow gates showed fresh tyre-marks. Steen was certainly around somewhere; it was just a question of waiting; and, in the meantime, fishing.

'I think the thing for these sort of conditions,' said Miles, 'is a swimfeeder.'

'Ah.'

'Yes. Quite definitely. Filled with a gentle and bread-paste mixture, with a couple of gentles on a number twelve hook, I think it'd be a cert for bream.'

'Maybe.'

'Yes. Or roach.'

'Hm.'

'Well, that's what it recommended in this angling magazine I was reading. I reckon these are the sort of conditions it described. More or less.'

'Yes.' Charles flipped his line out into the water. He'd been lent an old relegated rod with two mottled bamboo sections and a greenheart tip, a plastic centre-pin reel and a yellowed quill float. He'd put a couple of maggots on a small hook. He sat and watched the quill being borne along by the current and then leaning over as it tugged at the end of the swim.

'Have you plumbed?' asked Miles.

'I beg your pardon?'

'Plumbed the depth of the swim. You'll never catch anything if you don't do that. You see, what the angler has to do with his bait is to make it imitate as nearly as possible the conditions of nature. In nature things don't dangle awkwardly in the water. They flow, carried along by the current, a few inches above the bottom. Depending on the season, of course.'

'Of course.'

'Would you like a plummet? I've got one.'

'No thanks. I'm trying to give them up.'

Miles was silent, preoccupied with opening his latest piece of equipment. Proudly he stripped off the packaging and screwed a limp length of fibreglass to the end of his sleek fibreglass rod. Charles looked on with an expression of distaste which Miles took for admiration. 'Swingtip.'

'Ah.'

'Best sort of bite-detector for bottom-fishing.'

'Ah.' Charles reflected how Miles always talked out of books. His son-in-law was the least spontaneous person he'd ever met. Nothing came naturally; it all had to be worked at. Whatever interest he took up, he would begin by a painstaking study of the language and then buy all the correct equipment, before he actually did anything practical. Fishing was the latest accomplishment which Miles thought the young executive should not be without.

Again Charles found himself wondering about Miles and Juliet's sex-life. Had that been approached in the same meticulous way? 'Well, here we are on our honeymoon, Juliet darling. What I will do, when we are in bed and an atmosphere of mutual trust and relaxation has been established, is to practice a certain amount of foreplay. This is likely to begin with a kneading or massaging of the breasts in an accelerating stroking motion. This will be followed by manual clitoral stimulation . . .' The idea was intriguing. Charles wondered if he was becoming a dirty old man. But it *was* intriguing. Guiltily, he disguised his interest in a standard father-in-law question. 'Miles, have you and Juliet thought of having a family?'

Miles sat up with irritation. He'd just been trying to squeeze a split-shot on to his line and it had popped out of his fingers. 'Yes, Pop, we have. We reckon in about four and a half years I should have gone up at least a grade, so, allowing for the usual increments, and assuming that the mortgage rate doesn't rise above the present eleven per cent, I should think we could afford to let Juliet stop work then.'

There was no answer to that, so Charles sat and looked out over the water to Steen's bungalow. Nothing. It was very cold. The air stung his face and he felt the ground's iciness creep into his feet through the soles of Miles's relegated gum-boots. His body was stiff and uncomfortable. Always got like that when he sat still for a long time. He felt his years. A sure sign he needed a drink.

Miles had now completed the cat's cradle at the end of his line, and had loaded the perspex tube of his swim-feeder with a porridgy mash of bread and maggots. Two favoured maggots squirmed on the end of his size twelve hook (hooked, no doubt, as the books recommend, through the small vent in the thick end). Miles rose to his feet and fiddled with the knobs of his gleaming fixed-spool reel. 'The important thing,' he quoted almost to himself, 'is to remember it's not brute force with a fixed-spool reel; just a controlled flick.'

He made a controlled flick. The line jerked and maypoled itself around the rod. The contents of the swim-feeder sprayed from their case like shotgun pellets and landed with a scattering plop in the middle of the river. Charles didn't say anything, but controlled his lips and looked at his float. As he did so, it submerged. He struck, and reeled in rather a good perch.

Four hasty pints before the pub closed at two saw Charles through lunch, and there was a bit of wine too. 'Le Piat Beaujolais Primeur,' said Miles '—young, robust and slightly petillant, ideal with meat dishes.' (Obviously he had read a book on wine too.) The combination of alcohols anaesthetised Charles so that he could even watch the holiday slides of Tenerife without excessive pain.

They were not very varied—'Juliet in front of a shop . . . and here's Juliet in this bar place . . . and this one's of Juliet sitting on a rock . . . and here's Juliet in a boat—that was the day we went for a boat trip . . .' Obviously, Miles did not trust her with his camera or there might have been a matching sequence of 'Miles in front of a shop . . . Miles in this bar place . . .' etc. References in the commentary to shutter speeds, and exposures and lenses demonstrated that Miles had read a book on photography too. Charles let it all flow over him. Time was suspended, and he was too fuddled for darker thoughts.

The peaceful mood lasted until he stood alone on Goring Bridge. Miles and Juliet had offered him a lift to Pangbourne Station, but they'd got some people coming and were very relieved when he said he'd get a minicab to Reading. Miles had been dropping heavy hints about how difficult it was to get petrol and how he intended to use the Cortina 'for emergency uses only.' (By moving up from the level of salesman in his insurance company, he'd sacrificed a firm's car and was rather careful about using his own.)

When the cab came, Charles left in a surge of family effusiveness, and then, feeling like the hero of some of the terrible thriller films he'd been in during the fifties, he told the driver to go to Steen's home instead. As they approached Streatley, he lost his nerve and asked to be dropped by the bridge. The driver, with the predictability of all motorists over the last few weeks, commented on the petrol crisis, overcharged grossly, and drove off into the night.

The bridge at Goring is long and narrow; there are two spans to an island in the middle; one side is Streatley, the other Goring. Charles stood on the narrow pavement, leaning on the wooden parapet, and looked down into the water, which seemed infinitely deep in the darkness. Somewhere the church bells rang in the distance, calling the faithful to evensong. Their old-fashioned domesticity seemed incongruous as his thoughts darkened.

The pressure which had been building up all weekend was nearing some sort of explosion. The Steen business had to be sorted out that evening. Charles felt an uncomfortable sense of urgency. It was now nearly a week since Bill Sweet's death on Sunday 2nd December, and Jacqui was still in great danger. Charles had known the full implications of the situation for only twenty-four hours, but he had a sick feeling that time was running out. A sense of gloom blanketed his thought as he looked down to the dark water and heard the hiss of it rushing over the invisible weir ahead of him. Somewhere down in the depths, he felt certain, lay Marius Steen's gun, thrown away after the murder was committed.

He'd wasted the day. The fishing, the slides of Tenerife were all irrelevant; he should have been dealing with Steen. It was one of the most important responsibilities of his life. And this was one he couldn't shirk. It must be done straight away. He looked at his watch. Nearly seven. The pubs would soon be open. Just a quick drink for a bracer and then it must be done.

It was twenty past nine when he left the cosy fireside of the Bull. He was braced to the point of recklessness. Two hours of sipping Bell's and listening to the quacks of the local Scampi and Mateus Rosé crowd made the whole issue seem much simpler. If Steen was there, Charles had only to tell him the truth; if he wasn't, then he could leave the photographs with an anonymous note explaining Jacqui's innocence. He couldn't think why it hadn't occurred to him earlier, as he marched briskly (after a bit of trouble with the door latch) out of the pub.

The moon was fuller than the night before, but its light was diffused by cloud. He could see quite clearly as he climbed the hill out of the village. It didn't feel as cold as it had earlier in the day. He stopped to relieve himself into the roadside bushes and almost lost his balance as a car screeched round the corner in a clatter of gravel. He zipped himself up and strode onwards. A strange sense of purpose filled him, even a sense of honour. Sir Galahad nearing the end of his quest. Marius Steen, the giant who seemed to have been looming over his life now for a week was about to be confronted. A fragment repeated itself inappropriately like a *mantra* in Charles's mind. 'My strength is as the strength of ten, because my heart is pure.'

He was almost disappointed when he reached the gates. He'd expected a great brazen trumpet hanging, with a legend in outlandish characters—'Who dares to brave the giant's wrath, let him sound this trump.' And in the trees, clattering sadly, the armour of those who had dared, and failed in the combat. He turned to look at the trees, but they were bare. And the only sound was the wind breathing on their branches.

Charles leaned unsteadily against the gate-post and pressed the fluorescent button. He didn't wait for any response, but pushed open the heavy white gates with a scrunch of gravel. The bungalow again seemed to have grown in the moonlight, and was now a Moorish temple, where the infidel foe lurked. A light shone through a chink in the curtains of a window above the garage door.

No one appeared as Charles approached the front door, but he felt as if he was being watched. Suddenly the night had become very silent. He beat a tattoo with the doorknocker, and again its reverberations filled the whole world. But no one came. The quarry was lying low.

Charles pushed the door but it was very solid. He backed away and looked along the front of the house. The windows appeared to be shut firm. Garage? He walked heavily down the ramp and grasped the handle that should lift the door up and over. Locked.

But he had reached a pitch where he couldn't give up. He stumbled round the side of the house, through the flower beds, feeling the windows. All were tightly locked.

Round the back of the bungalow he was suddenly aware of the slow wash of water at the end of the lawn. There was no other sound and no light was visible on this elevation. But he knew Marius Steen was inside.

There was a small door which corresponded with the back of the garage. He walked up a crazy-paving path and tried the handle. Braced for a shove he nearly overbalanced when the door gave inwards.

It was very dark. He blinked, trying to accustom his eyes to the change, but still couldn't see much. There were no windows and only a trickle of light came in through the door behind him. From what he could see, it illuminated a pile of boxes. Perhaps he was in some sort of storeroom rather than the garage. He moved slowly forward, groping ahead with a breast-stroke motion.

But discretion was difficult in his alcoholic state. There was something in the way of his foot, then an object with a sharp edge fell agonisingly onto his ankle. Whatever it was precipitated an avalanche of other objects which thundered down around him as Charles fell sprawling to the ground.

He lay frozen, waiting for some reaction, but there was nothing. It was only his tense state that made the crash sound so loud. Gingerly, he reached forward, found a wall and levered himself up against it. Then he felt along to a door frame and followed its outline until he found a light-switch.

The sudden glare was blinding, but when he unscrewed his eyes, he could see he was in a kind of windowless utility room. There was a washing machine, a spin dryer, a washing-up machine, a deep-freeze and rows of neatly hanging brooms and mops. Above these was a cluster of meters, fuse-boxes and power-switches. Deep shelves on the opposite wall contained boxes of tinned food and crates of spirits. There was a spreading honeycomb of a wine-rack, full and expensive-looking.

And on the floor Charles could see what had caused his fall. A pile of boxes lay scattered like a demolished chimney. He knelt down and re-piled them. They were heavy, as he knew from the numbing pain in his shin. He looked at the writing on the boxes. 'Salmon,' 'Trout,' 'Strawberries.' 'Do not refreeze.' Marius Steen certainly knew how to live.

When he had finished piling the boxes up, Charles looked once more round the room and his eyes lighted on the very thing he needed at that moment—a torch. It was a long, black, rubber-encased one, hanging from a hook by the back door. He took it down, switched on, turned off the light and opened the door into the rest of the house.

He was in the garage. It was large, but dominated by the huge form of a dark blue Rolls-Royce. Remembering a detail with sudden clarity, Charles knelt down and looked at the left-hand side of the front bumper. There was a little dent, which he'd lay any money corresponded to the dent in the back right-hand wing of Bill Sweet's Ford Escort. The door of the Rolls was not locked. Key in the ignition, nothing in the glove compartment and the petrol gauge read empty.

Charles moved round the great car, looking for any other clues it might give. He felt his foot slip under him and sat down with a jarring shock, landing uncomfortably on a spanner and a piece of plastic tubing. Fate seemed determined to translate his dramatic mission into slapstick.

He found the door which led to the body of the house, along a corridor and into the large hall. All the walls were hung with hunting prints which were anonymously expensive, bought on advice by a man without natural taste. Two enormous china Dalmatians stood guarding the front door. They seemed to reflect more of their owner's personality. They were Steen the showman; the prints were Steen the man who wanted to gatecrash high society, the man who wanted a knighthood.

There were no lights in evidence, except for a slight

glow from the top of a short flight of steps, which must lead to a room above the garage. The room whose light Charles had seen from the front.

He moved purposefully up the stairs and began to feel faint. The drink was telling; he felt his energy wane. He had to get the interview over quickly.

The first room he came to was a kind of study, equipped with telephones, typewriters, and copying machines. The walls were covered with framed photographs of stars from Marius Steen's shows, scribbled with effusive messages. It was a sentimental showbiz touch that again didn't fit the man's character. What he felt was wanted, rather than what he wanted. Bernard Walton's face grinned patronisingly down from the wall.

The study was empty; the light came from the adjacent room. Charles switched off his torch with a dull click and moved towards the half-open door. Through its crack he could see a plush bedroom, dominated by a large four-poster bed. Curtains obscured his view, but the shape of the covers told him that the bed was occupied.

As he entered the room, exhaustion threatened to swamp him, but still he moved forward. Now, in the light of a bedside lamp, he could see Marius Steen lying back on the pillows asleep. The great beak of a nose, familiar from countless press photographs, rose out of the sheets like the dorsal fin of a shark. One large hand lay, palm upward, on the cover.

'Wake him, tell him and go.' Charles formulated his thoughts very simply with desperate concentration. He staggered forward to the bedside and stood there, swaying. As he reached for Steen's hand, he heard a car drawing up outside the gates. He clutched at the hand in panic, and felt the coldness of death.

CHAPTER NINE

INTERVAL

Charles woke as if his body was being dragged out of a deep pit, and memory returned slowly to his pounding head. He didn't like it when it came. He could see Steen's face in its pained repose, and felt certain that he was up against a case of murder.

He was lying in bed in Miles and Juliet's spare room. Vague memories of getting there. The rush from Steen's bedroom out through the garage and utility room, as he heard a car stopping on the gravel and footsteps approaching the garage door. Then he remembered skulking breathless behind the bungalow until the car was safely garaged, a rush through the gates, staggering along the road till a police car stopped, warnings—'Had a few too many, haven't you, sir? Still, won't charge you this time. But watch it'—and ignominious delivery on Miles and Juliet's doorstep.

He heaved himself out of bed and limped downstairs. The bruise on his ankle was cripplingly painful and he felt his forty-seven years. Too old to be involved in this escalating round of violence.

Juliet stood staring at him as he made it to the kitchen chair. She appeared not to have inherited Frances's forgiving nature. 'Really, Daddy, what a state to come home in.'

'I'm sorry, love.'

'Miles was furious.'

'Oh well.' There were more important things than Miles's sensibilities.

'I mean, the police coming here. What will other people on the estate think?'

'You can tell them the police weren't coming for you or Miles.'

'They wouldn't think that!'

'Miles can tell them it's just his drunken father-in-law.'

'I don't think they'd find that very amusing.' She turned away to make coffee. 'Honestly, Daddy, I don't think you have any concept of human dignity.'

That hurt. 'Listen, Juliet *darling*. I think I probably have more knowledge of the really important things that give a person dignity than . . .' But it wasn't worth explaining; she wouldn't understand. 'Oh, forget it. Shouldn't you be at work?'

'I'm not going in till after lunch. There's not much to do and . . . well, I was worried about you.'

It was the first softening Charles could ever remember hearing from Juliet. It warmed him. 'Thank you.'

'Honestly, Daddy, I don't know what you're up to half the time. That peculiar phone-call yesterday morning, and now all this. What on earth were you doing in Streatley anyway? I thought you had taken the cab to Reading.'

'Yes, I know. The thing is, I had to change my plans. It's all rather involved, but . . .' He paused, and all the boiling thoughts inside him strained for an outlet. He had to tell someone. Why not Juliet? 'Marius Steen is dead.'

'Yes, I know.' Her answer was cool and unconcerned.

'How do you know?'

'It was on the radio this morning. On the *Today* programme.'

'What? How did it say he died?'

'Heart attack, I think it was. Here's your coffee.' As she placed the cup in front of him, Charles looked at his daughter, wondering if she could be involved in this grotesque business. But in her face, as easily read as her mother's, there was nothing devious; she was telling the truth. 'Anyway, Daddy, why do you tell me that? Was it Steen you went to see last night?'

'No.'

'I didn't know you knew him.'

'I didn't.' He sipped the coffee. It wasn't what he needed. His body felt dangerously unstable and bilious. 'Juliet, could you get me a drop of whisky?'

'At this time in the morning? Daddy'—with all the awe of a television documentary—'are you an alcoholic?'

'I don't know. I've never thought about it. Where does liking a drink stop and being an alcoholic start?'

'I should think it starts when you need a *hair of the dog* the next morning.' Juliet italicised the unfamiliar phrase.

'Well, I do need one now.'

'I don't know whether I should—'

'Oh, get it!' he snapped impatiently. As Juliet scurried shocked to the cocktail cabinet, Charles asked himself whether he was in fact an alcoholic. On balance, he decided he probably wasn't. He could do without drink. But he wouldn't like to have to. It was an old joke—a teetotaller knows every morning when he wakes up that that's the best he's going to feel all day. Drink at least offers some prospect of things improving.

He felt Juliet's shocked eyes on him as he poured whisky into his coffee and drank it gratefully. It made him feel more stable, but desperately tired. Waves of relief washed over him. Steen had died of a heart attack. Thoughts of murder had been prompted only by the events of the previous week and the melodramatic circumstances of the discovery of the body. All the contradictory details evaporated. Charles believed what he wanted to believe. The pressure was off. 'Juliet love, what's the time?'

'Twenty past ten.'

'Look, I think I'll go back to bed for a bit.'

'But you must have something to eat.' Frances's eternal cry.

'When have you got to go to work?'

'Have to leave quarter to two.'

'Wake me at half-past twelve. Then I'll have something to eat. I promise.'

It wasn't until after lunch and Juliet's departure that Charles remembered about Jacqui, still lying low at Hereford Road. The public announcement of Steen's death had sapped the urgency out of him and yesterday's imperatives no longer mattered. Jacqui was just the frayed end of an otherwise completed pattern and it was with reluctance that he dialled his own number.

Jacqui answered. All of the Swedish girls must be out at their various Swedish employments. Her voice was guarded, but not panic-stricken. 'Charles? I wondered when you were going to ring. I was just about to leave.'

'Jacqui, I've got some bad news . . .'

'It's all right. I heard. On *Open House*.'

'What?'

'The radio.'

'Ah. Well, I'm sorry.'

'Thank you.' There was a pause, and Charles could feel how fiercely she was controlling her emotions.

'Jacqui, I'm afraid I never got the photos to him.'

'That hardly matters now, does it? Nothing much matters now.'

'Jacqui . . .'

'I'll be all right.'

'Yes. I suppose that's the end of it, isn't it?'

'I wouldn't count on that.'

'What do you mean?' Charles had an unpleasant feeling he was about to sacrifice his recently-won calm.

'Do you think he died of a heart attack, Charles?'

'Yes.'

There was a grunt from the other end of the line, a sound between exasperation and despair. 'Charles, I can't talk about it now. I'm too . . . I'll talk when—'

'Tomorrow?'

'Yes, if I feel OK. Come round when you . . . Evening. Eight or . . .'

'OK I'll be there. Archer Street. You'll be all right now?'

'Like hell.' The phone went dead.

Before Charles left the house in Pangbourne, he took the envelope of photographs out of his inside pocket and looked at them. With Steen's death they had changed. Already they had the air of curios or souvenirs—oddities from another age. The erotic quality had drained from them and they seemed like sepia prints in an album of someone else's relations. Mildly interesting, but ultimately irrelevant.

He looked around for somewhere to destroy them. The trouble with architect-designed houses on estates is that they have nothing like an open fire. The central heating was fired by oil. (Miles had already spoken gloomily of the inevitable price rises which the Middle East situation must precipitate. As he said portentously, 'You know, Pop, the days of cheap fuel are over.') The cooker was electric. There was no convenient stove to consume the evidence.

Charles took a giant box of matches from the kitchen and went out into the garden. The forty-foot-long area was neatly organised. A potting shed of conspicuous new timber, a patio area protected by a screen of lattice-work bricks, a path of very sane crazy-paving winding diagonally across the lawn, a meticulous row of cloches. Only the winter shagginess of the grass gave any hint of rampant nature or humanity.

It had started to rain. Big heavy drops that were cold as they fell, penetrating, on his head and shoulders. In the far corner of the garden Charles saw what he was looking for. Neatly screened by another low wall of lattice-work bricks were a compost heap, bound in by wooden slats, and an empty metal incinerator. He lit the photographs one by one and let the flimsy black rectangles of ash drop into the bin. Finally he burnt the envelope, then stirred the dampening fragments into a black unrecognisable mash.

CHAPTER TEN

SECOND ACT BEGINNERS

The obituary appeared in *The Times* the next day, Tuesday 11th December.

MR MARIUS STEEN
Impresario and Showman

Mr Marius Steen, CBE, the impresario, died on Sunday. He was 68. Born in Warsaw in 1905, his full name was Marius Ladislas Steniatowski, but he shortened it for convenience when his parents came to England in 1921. His father was a tailor and for some years the young Steen helped him in his business. But already the attraction of entertainment was strong; Steen spent most of his limited pocket-money on tickets for the music hall and in 1923 launched himself as Mario, the Melodic Whistler. In spite of changes in name and act, he was never a success as a performer, but became increasingly interested in the business of promotion and management. The first act he managed was Herbert and his Horrible Dogs in 1924.

Soon he was progressing from individual acts to the presentation of complete shows. Though he started with wrestling and all-girl revues, by 1930 he was presenting variety bills at music halls all over the country. Through the Thirties he centralised his activities on London and, in 1935, had his first major success with the spectacular revue *Go with the Girls*. None of these early productions had a great deal to recommend them artistically, but Steen always maintained that success must be measured by public reaction alone. And by that criterion his shows were highly successful.

Steen continued presenting revues, with an increasing reliance on scripted comedy rather than just dancing girls, until the outbreak of war. Then he moved into the cinema and, with his customary unflagging energy, set up a series of films in keeping with the jingoistic spirit of the times. Of these the most memorable was *Brothers in Battledress*, directed by William Hankin.

After the war Marius Steen continued to put on shows and gradually he forsook revue for musicals and light comedies. *What's in the Box?* was one of the greatest successes of 1953, and in 1960 Steen's purchase of the King's Theatre off Shaftesbury Avenue heralded a string of commercial triumphs, including *One Thing After Another*, which ran for three years, and, currently, *Sex of One and Half a Dozen of the Other*.

Steen maintained his interest in the cinema and put money into many ventures including the highly successful Steenway Productions, which makes horror films. He was also a major shareholder in three commercial television companies, and was at the time of his death interesting himself in the production of programmes for network on the new commercial radio station.

Marius Steen was often criticised for his healthy disrespect for 'Art' and there are many stories of this supposed philistinism which he loved to tell against himself. (On first hearing of Michelangelo, he is reputed to have asked 'Michael who?' His alleged description of opera as 'fat gits singing' is probably apocryphal.) He was a forthright man who made enemies, but was loved and respected by his friends. He had no hobbies, maintaining that if a person needed hobbies, then there was something wrong with his work. He divided his time between his houses in London and Streatley and a villa in the South of France. In 1969 he was awarded the CBE for services to the theatre.

Marius Steen married Rose Whittle in 1934. She died in 1949 and he never remarried. He leaves a son.

Charles was impressed. It was quite an achievement for anyone in the theatre to command that many column inches in *The Times*. The obituary seemed like a washing of the body. It cleaned Steen up. The existence of the photographs, all the sordid aspects of the man's life were rinsed away by the formalised prose. The Western ritual of death was observed—the obligation to remember the most dignified image of the deceased. Like those ghastly American mausoleums where the embalmed corpse is presented at its best, dressed and smiling, prior to burial. But Charles had a nagging feeling that, however Marius Steen was tarted up in death, his corpse would not lie down.

Charles arrived at the Archer Street flat with a two-litre bottle of Valpolicella from Oddbins and a determination to be very slow on the uptake in any discussion of Steen's death. Jacqui looked ghastly when she opened the door. Her face was pale and her eyes were puffy red slits.

'Are you all right?'

'I will be, Charles. I'll just sit down for a moment.'

'Can I get you a drink?'

'No. It'd make me sick. But help yourself.'

The events of the last few days had made Charles forget about Jacqui's flat being done over, but inside it the evidence was all too clear. She had obviously made some attempt to tidy up. There were two cardboard boxes in the middle of the room full of bits of glass and torn clothes. But the curtains were still hanging shredded from their rails, and the bed smelt of oil from the smashed lamp. The little room looked sad and crippled.

He didn't make any comment, but found an unbroken glass and filled it with Valpolicella. 'Do you want to go out to eat, Jacqui?'

'No, I couldn't.'

'Hmm.' The silence was obtrusive. Feebly he repeated himself. 'Do you feel all right?'

'Charles, the bloke I loved and whose kid I've got has just been murdered.'

'I'm sorry.' He stolidly avoided reacting to the word 'murdered.' Jacqui softened. 'I'll get you some food later. When I can face it.'

'Don't worry about that. Not particularly hungry.'

'No.' Again they were conscious of the silence. Then Jacqui burst out. 'He always was a little sod.'

Charles was genuinely amazed. 'Who?'

'Nigel.'

'Nigel Steen?'

'Well, who else?'

'Why do you suddenly bring him in?'

'Because he killed Marius, that's why.'

This new direction of thought was too sudden for Charles to take in. Deliberately, he slowed down. 'What on earth do you mean? You haven't got any reason for saying that.'

'Of course I have. Who else stood to get anything out of Marius's death?'

'I don't know. I would have thought Nigel was doing all right anyway. He didn't need to murder anyone. Presumably he'd have got everything when his father went. He only had to wait.'

'He's greedy. Anyway, things may have changed. Maybe he had to move fast.'

'What do you mean?' Charles asked patiently, determined to humour her through this crazy new idea.

'Marius was thinking of changing his will in favour of me and the baby.'

'Oh yes.' Charles tried to sound believing, but failed.

'Yes, he bloody was. He was even talking about us getting married.'

'When was this?'

'First in the South of France. Then when I told him about the baby he was more definite. He said he'd felt awful about the abortion last time, and he wanted to keep this one and marry me and start again.'

'And cut Nigel out of the will?'

'I suppose so.'

It didn't sound very plausible. Even if Steen had ever had such intentions, the events of the last week made it clear that he had changed his mind. And the whole idea of remarriage and disowning Nigel was the sort of novelette situation that would appeal to Jacqui. Still, he couldn't be completely brutal with her. 'Why didn't you mention this before?'

'It was a secret. Between Marius and me. It was all going to be secret. Even when we married it was going to be a secret for a bit. But now he's dead . . .' She broke down.

Charles calmed her and forced her to drink a little wine. But when she was composed again, he felt he had to be cruel. If Steen had been murdered (and he had no cause to believe that that was the case), then it was something to do with the Sweets and the blackmailing business. It was dangerous for Jacqui to go around blaming his son. She was quite capable of going to the police and making accusations which, since she hadn't a shred of evidence, could only lead to trouble. This nonsense had to be stopped.

'If what you say is true, how do you explain Steen's behaviour during the past week? Hardly the actions of a devoted husband-to-be.'

He could see from her face that that really hurt, and also that it was something she hadn't been able to work out satisfactorily for herself. 'Well, Nigel kept him from me. Marius went off to Berkshire—where he didn't want to be disturbed. He'd often do that,' she added defensively, 'go off with a great pile of scripts, looking for his next show. And then Nigel left all those messages for me.'

'And he sent the note?'

'Yes.'

'Pity I burnt it. Wc could have got the handwriting analysed,' he said skeptically.

'That note's just the sort of thing the little sod would do.'

'Jacqui, why, if Nigel had decided to kill his father anyway, did he bother to give the impression you were out of favour?'

'So that, when he'd done it, nobody would believe me when I said about us getting married. They'd think we'd had a quarrel.'

It was ingenious, but Charles didn't feel very inclined to accept the reasoning. 'All right then, when did Nigel do the murder?'

'Sunday evening. When he says he found the body.'

'How do you know he found the body? It wasn't in the papers.'

'I rang Morrison. He told me.'

'Who's Morrison?'

'Sort of odd-job man at Orme Gardens. He was meant to be the chauffeur, but Marius liked driving himself. I rang Morrison and he told me Nigel had driven down to Streatley and found the body dead in bed at about quarter past eleven on Sunday night. Well, Marius never went to bed before one, so I don't believe that for a start.'

'I think you may have to believe it.' Charles told her

about his movements on the Sunday night, concluding, '. . . so it must have been the arrival of Nigel's car that made me run out of the place.'

'And you are sure Marius was dead?'

'Quite sure. He was cold. He had been dead some time.'

'Perhaps Nigel had come earlier and killed him and then arranged to come back and find the body.'

'I hate to sound like a detective, but there was a puddle outside the front gate and only one new set of tyre-marks between the Saturday night and the Sunday night. They must have been Steen coming back on the Saturday. I know he did come back because of the new tape on the Ansaphone.'

'Perhaps Nigel killed him on the Saturday night.' Jacqui was desperate to hang on to her theory, but she could feel it slipping away. Charles shook his head. 'I'm sorry, Jacqui, but you must face the facts. Marius had a history of heart trouble—you say he'd had a minor attack before you went to France in the summer. He was a man of 68—worked hard all his life—never made any concessions to age. Is it surprising that he should die a natural death from a heart attack? Apart from anything else, if there were suspicious circumstances, the doctor wouldn't have signed a certificate. So far as we know there's been no suspicion of foul play.'

'The doctor must have been in league with Nigel,' Jacqui insisted truculently.

'If there was any mark on the body, the undertaker would notice.'

'There are poisons which don't leave any trace.'

'Jacqui, my love'—he deliberately sounded patronising. Having chosen the role of the infinitely reasonable older man, he was determined to stick to it—'you have read too many detective stories.'

That finally silenced her. She sat still for a full five

minutes, then stood up brusquely. 'I'll get you some food.'

It was another of Jacqui's frozen meals. This time fish steaks with still-frozen centres and bright slivers of French beans. Charles consumed most of the Valpolicella and tried to steer the conversation away from anything to do with Marius Steen. It was difficult. Small talk kept erupting into some new accusation or burst of crying from Jacqui. Charles found it a strain and was relieved when the meal was over and he felt he could decently leave. 'You get to bed, Jacqui. You look absolutely knackered. I'd better be off.'

'Yes. Charles.'

'Yes.'

'Do you mind staying?'

'No. OK.' He lied. She obviously needed him, and so the awkwardness must be prolonged.

'I don't mean . . . you know . . .' she said feebly, and the waif-like expression on her strained face made it difficult to grasp immediately what she did mean. Then he realised she was referring to sex. It seemed incongruous in relation to the events of the last week.

'Of course not. No, I'll stay. As long as you need someone around.'

'Just for the night. I didn't sleep at all last night. It was awful. I kept hearing things and imagining. Just tonight. I'll be all right tomorrow. Got to be. Sort out what I'm going to do about the baby. I'll have to get rid of it.'

'Jacqui, you must keep the baby.' Charles had long since ceased to delude himself that he had any immovable principles on anything, but he felt something approaching that on the subject of abortion. Without having a particular reason, like Catholicism, he found it unjustifiable. He tried to argue in his mind against this conviction, because he was frightened by feelings of such strength. Granted, he'd say to himself, I've never been in a situation where an abortion has been necessary. Natural caution has prevented me from getting anyone into trouble. If it happened, no doubt that principle would crumble like any other. But the instinct remained strong.

And as Jacqui's suffering face looked up at him, he knew he had said the right thing. There was relief and determination there, in spite of her words. 'But I can't look after a baby on my own. I can hardly look after myself.'

She sounded so plaintive that Charles laughed and Jacqui even managed a brief grin. 'Don't worry'—at his most avuncular—'something'll happen.'

'What? Nothing can, now Marius is dead.'

'Something will happen,' he repeated with a confidence whose basis he didn't like to investigate. 'Now, where am I going to sleep?'

'Oh, with me. It's daft for you to get a stiff neck on the sofa when there's room in my bed.'

So they settled down, Charles in shirt and underpants, Jacqui in silk pyjamas, cradled in his arms. It was eight days since they had last lain on the bed together, and sex seemed as far away now as then. But this time Charles's feelings were mellower. It seemed all right that this sad and trembling body should lie in his arms. There was a lot to be said for cuddling. Now he seemed to find it even more attractive than screwing. Perhaps it was the approach of old age, sliding into impotent fumblings. As he fell asleep, Byron's lines floated through his fuddled mind.

We'll go no more a-screwing
So late into the night,
Though the heart is still as loving
And the moon is still as bright.

* * *

When he woke, he was alone in the bed. He could hear Jacqui being sick in the bathroom. It was a nostalgic sound, taking him back to the flat in Notting Hill where he and Frances had started their married life; and started Juliet; and, in a way, started living apart. Nappies boiling on the gas-stove, the sweet smell of breast milk—it all came back. 'I am degenerating into a sentimental old fool,' he thought as he rolled out of bed.

Jacqui came in as he was pulling on his trousers, and sat down, looking drained. 'OK?' he asked.

'I will be. I hope I will. It's ghastly. Look.' She closed her eyes grimly and pointed at the table. There was a letter which had been opened and shoved back into the envelope.

'Can I read it?' Jacqui nodded. Charles pulled the papers out. There was a short letter and a smaller envelope, which had also been opened. The letter was on paper headed 'Cohn, Jarvis, Cohn and Stickley—Solicitors and Commissioners for Oaths.'

Dear Miss Mitchell,

On the instructions of my client, Mr Marius Steen, I am sending you the enclosed letter. I have no knowledge of its contents, but was instructed to send it to you as soon as I heard news of Mr Steen's death.

Yours sincerely,
Harold Cohn

'Can I read the other one?'

'Go ahead.'

He opened the envelope. The letter was written in a sprawling hand, writing that had once undergone the discipline of copperplate, but long ago broken loose from its restrictions and now spread, thick and unguarded, over the page.

2nd November

Dear Titty . . .

Jacqui was studying Charles's face and anticipating his reaction. 'Marius always called me that.' Charles continued reading.

If you get this letter, I am dead. So I'm sorry. The old heart or some other bit of my body has given out and fouled the system and I've gone. So that's a pity. Not because I haven't had a good run, just that I'd like the run to continue. I'm a winner and I want to go on winning. And when you came on the scene, I started enjoying my winning even more.

As you know, I wanted to marry you. Depending on when you get this letter, I may already have married you. If not, believe me, it's all I want to do. I only care about you and the little bastard in your belly. I'm sure he'll turn out better than the other one.

And the main purpose of this letter is to tell you and your beautiful body not to worry. If Marius is dead, Marius will still look after you. There'll be money for you and the baby. Call him Marius.

Love,
Marius

Charles looked up at Jacqui. In her face was discomfort and sadness, but also an unmistakable gleam of triumph.

CHAPTER ELEVEN

ENTER THE FUNNY POLICEMAN

He thought he must be going soft in the head. To have tried to help Jacqui in the matter of the photographs was illogical, but at least generous, getting her out of an awkward situation. But assisting her investigations into a perfectly natural death as if it were murder was little short of lunacy.

She had read so much into Steen's letter. Channelling all the pain of her loss into arguments to support her theory, she leapt on to the promise of provision for her and the baby, and to the sentence, 'I'm sure he'll turn out better than the other one.' To her mind, these proved conclusively that Marius had decided to change his will in her favour, and that Nigel had got wind of this and forestalled his father's plans by killing him. Charles put up all the arguments skepticism could muster, but somehow ended up agreeing with Jacqui that it was at least worth further investigation.

Which was why, on Thursday 13th December, he was taking Gerald Venables out to lunch. Gerald had been a contemporary at Oxford, who had read Law and acted a little. He had been elected Treasurer of the Oxford University Dramatic Society and, as such, demonstrated the prime motive of his life—an unashamed love of money. This motive led him after university away from the Theatre and into the Law. He joined a firm of solicitors specialising in show-business contract work, became a partner within five years and thereafter just made more and more money. The subject fascinated him; he always talked about money; but did it with such an ingenuous enthusiasm that the effect was not alienating. At worst he was boring, in the same way that a golfer or a photographer or a dinghy-sailor or any other person obsessed by a hobby is boring.

When the Stilton was produced, Gerald undid another button of his exquisitely cut tweed waistcoat and patted his paunch beneficently. 'What is it, Charles? Are you putting some work my way? I'd better warn you, my rates, which were always pretty high, are now almost beyond belief.'

'I anticipated as much. It's not exactly work. I don't know how you'd define it . . .'

'Ah, if it isn't readily defined, it's automatically at double the rate.'

'Yes. It's a matter of investigation—or do I mean snooping?'

'That's what solicitors are for.'

'Exactly. The point is, I know solicitors individually are totally immoral'—Gerald nodded assent as if accepting a compliment—'and I suppose, as with any other bunch of thieves, there is honour among you.' Again Gerald graciously inclined his head. 'So no doubt you scratch each other's backs.' The third nod was very positive. 'What I want you to do is to find out some information from another solicitor.'

'Officially?'

'Unofficially.'

'Ah. Comes more expensive.'

'I thought it might.'

'What do you want to know, Charles?'

'You've heard of Marius Steen, bloke who's just died?'

'Of course. Been involved in a lot of contracts with him. He was a real shark, totally immoral.' Gerald's voice carried a hint of respect as he made this tribute.

'So you know his solicitor?'

'Harold Cohn. Of course. He's the hardest bargainer

in the business.' A diffident smile. 'Present company, of course, excepted.'

'Of course.'

'And you want to know about the old man's will?'

'How the hell did you know that?'

'Because there's nothing else anyone could possibly want to know about a man three days dead. There has been quite a lot of speculation on the matter in professional circles.'

'Any conclusions?'

'Rumours, but nothing definite.'

'Do you think you could find out?'

Gerald smiled blandly. 'I wouldn't have thought it was beyond the realms of possibility.' A waiter was hovering at his shoulder. 'We'll have coffee, won't we, Charles? And a Cognac, perhaps. Yes, two Cognacs.' He looked thoughtfully over the table. 'Now I wonder why you would be interested in Steen's will, Charles. You're hardly expecting to be a beneficiary, are you?'

'No. Hardly.'

Gerald looked at him, puzzled. He didn't like being in a position of ignorance on any subject, and started probing. 'Whoever it goes to, there's a lot.'

'Yes.'

'Steen did all right. Even with estate duty, it'll be worth having.'

Charles nodded, determined not to give anything away. Gerald tried another tack. 'You want to find this out for yourself?'

'Yes.'

'It'll be public knowledge soon. If you can only wait a few—'

'I want to know as soon as possible.'

'Well, Charles, you are a dark horse.' Gerald sat back in his chair and sipped his Cognac. It was amusing for Charles to see him in this state, his usual poise unbalanced by childlike curiosity. 'Charles, is it a crime?'

'What do you mean?'

'Are there any suspicions about the will? Surprise heirs in Australia, forgery, skulduggery with birth certificates, secret codicils?' Gerald threw out the ideas like baits, hoping to catch some reaction. Charles smiled in a way that he knew was infuriating.

Gerald was suitably infuriated. 'Oh, for God's sake, Charles. You can tell me. Look, if I know the circumstances, it'll make my enquiries much easier.' Charles continued to smile. Gerald was reduced to infantile tactics. 'Listen, if you don't tell me why you want to know, then I won't find out for you.'

'Oh dear. Then I'll have to ask someone else.'

Gerald looked rattled, but controlled himself, smiled and said, 'Charles, if there's anything suspicious, I want to know. Look, I'm a sucker for that sort of thing. Always reading detective stories. I don't know, it's a fascination. It's my hobby, if you like.'

'I thought your hobby was money.'

'That's my main one, but I can't resist suspicious circumstances. It's been a life-long ambition of mine to be involved in something mysterious, a crime. I don't mean the sort of official crime I deal with as a solicitor. I mean real cloak-and-dagger investigation stuff.' Charles remained silent. 'Listen, if you are involved in crime, from whatever side of the law, you need a solicitor. Oh, Charles, do tell me!' he burst out petulantly, but still got no reaction. 'Listen, if you are investigating a crime—'

'And what on earth makes you think I am?'

'I don't know. Something about the way you're behaving. Listen, if you are, I won't charge you anything.'

'You what?'

'I will undertake any investigations free . . .'

'Gerald, are you feeling all right?'

'. . . so long as you let me in on all the details.'

'Hmm.' Charles was circumspect. It was a very good offer, an amazing offer, considering who it came from. But he himself felt so far from convinced there was any crime to investigate, that he had no desire to spread ill-founded suspicions. 'Gerald,' he began slowly, 'if there were something fishy, and I were to tell you, could I trust your discretion?'

'Of course.' Gerald was affronted. 'I am a solicitor.'

'That's what I mean. All right, I accept your offer.'

'So there is a crime?'

'Maybe.'

'All right, give me the dirt.' Gerald made no pretence of maturity now. He was an eager child. Charles remembered that Gerald had always been like that. It was the same quality that made his fascination with money so inoffensive. Not for the first time Charles reflected that growing-up is a myth; getting older is just an intenser form of childhood. 'I'll give you the dirt,' he said, denying the child his treat, 'when you tell me about the will.'

'You bugger,' said Gerald. But he agreed to the deal.

When the bill was brought to Charles, it was enormous. It was a long time since he'd eaten out in this style and he was shocked by the escalation of prices and VAT. 'Think yourself lucky,' said Gerald, as Charles counted out the notes. 'It we hadn't come to an agreement, you'd be paying for my time as well.'

Charles didn't tell Jacqui about their new ally in investigation when they met up that evening to report progress. He just said he'd met his solicitor friend who reckoned he could find out the details of the will.

Jacqui was in quite a state. She'd been down to Goring for Marius's funeral (having found out the time by ringing Morrison at Orme Gardens). At the church she'd ended up in the cliché situation of being frozen out by Marius's relatives. It was the stereotyped picture beloved of cartoonists—the family (Nigel and a few cousins), trim in their black on one side of the grave, and the floozy (Jacqui), in an unsuitable black cocktail dress and purple fur-collared coat, weeping on the other. The burial had been a small affair. Marius was against cremation; he wanted to lie in an English grave with a marble headstone. A memorial service in St George's, Hanover Square, was to follow, for Steen's theatrical and business acquaintances. No one spoke to Jacqui or even acknowledged her, except for Morrison. By the end of the ceremony she was so upset that she hadn't the nerve to go to the house with the small party of mourners, and caught a train straight back to London.

However, she had managed to have a few brief words with Morrison and questioned him about Nigel's movements over the weekend of his father's death. (She assured Charles she had been subtle in her questioning, but he dreaded to think what she meant by subtlety. If there were any alarms to start, he had no doubt she'd set them jangling). From Morrison she had found out a significant fact, which would have deterred anyone less prejudiced in their conviction of Nigel Steen's guilt. The young man's car, a Jensen Interceptor, was out of action at the relevant time. It had had brake trouble and Morrison, who was an expert mechanic, had offered to mend it over the weekend. He'd attended to the brakes on the Saturday, but then, feeling unhappy with the alignment of the wheels, had started work on them. He was a perfectionist, and the job took a long time. When he left the vehicle on the Saturday evening, all four wheels were off, and they were in that state when he returned to the job on the Sunday morning. He didn't finish work until the evening, and it was then that Nigel drove off down to Berkshire, and found his father dead. In reply to the question as to whether Nigel could have used the Datsun, Morrison couldn't say. Miss Menzies had filled it with petrol on the Friday afternoon and used it on the Monday morning. No doubt she would have noticed if it had been used in the interim.

'Who's Miss Menzies?' asked Charles.

'Joanne. Marius's secretary.'

'Oh yes. I've met her. Hmm. And you actually managed to get all that information without Morrison getting at all suspicious?'

'Yes. Anyway, what if he did get suspicious? He doesn't like Nigel any more than anyone else.'

It seemed to be a feature of the case that no one had a good word to say for Nigel Steen. Not having met the man, and basing his conclusions on other people's prejudices, Charles decided that young Steen's main offence was that he was not his father. From all accounts he didn't sound as if he had the spunk to be a murderer.

'Where does Nigel live?'

'I think he's got a flat near Knightsbridge, but he's never there. Spends all his time in Orme Gardens or at Streatley.'

'Father's boy?'

'I wouldn't say that.'

'How did they get on, Jacqui?'

'I don't know. I hardly ever saw them together, and Marius never talked about Nigel. But you've seen the letter.'

'Yes. And did Joanne like him?'

'Did she like who? She liked Marius.' Was there a hint of jealousy there?

'No. Nigel.'

'I don't think she liked him.'

'Hmm. Then I think perhaps she's due for a visitation.'

* * *

Charles was making-up next morning in Hereford Road when the phone rang.

'Hello. Oh, Maurice, I was just making-up.'

'What for? You working and not telling me?'

'No, just for fun. Practice.'

'Well, I think it's about time you did some work. You seem to have taken the three-day week to heart too quickly.'

'Three-day week?'

'Don't you read the papers?'

'I haven't yet this morning.'

'Heath's going to put the whole country on a three-day week. Save power. And stop television at half-past ten in the evening.'

'Really.'

'Yes. Think of all the ten per cents of all those series I won't be getting. Johnny Wilson had a repeat scheduled for late evening. That'll be off.'

'I'm afraid I'm not very in touch.'

'I'll say. Look, you know that *Softly Softly* I said might be coming up?'

'Yes.'

'Well, it hasn't.'

'Oh. Thanks.'

'But there is something. Had a call from the casting director of a new horror film yesterday. They're looking for someone to play this sort of deformed hunchback, part werewolf, part vampire. I told them you were made for the part.'

'Thank you very much.'

Silence punctuated with gasps from the other end of the line showed that Maurice was roaring with laughter at his own witticism. He always laughed noiselessly, his jaw snapping up and down as he took in great gulps of air. Charles waited until he'd recovered sufficiently to continue.

'Sorry, just a little joke. But really, it is that sort of part. They seemed quite keen when I mentioned you. Said "Yes, we like using the old fifties stars everyone's forgotten."'

'Thank you again. What would it involve?'

'Two weeks' filming early January—if this three-day week nonsense doesn't interfere. At some stately home. Forget where exactly, but within reach of London.'

'Hmm. What's the film called?'

'The Zombie Walks!'

'Oh God. Who's directing?'

'Never heard of him. Some name like Rissole. It's being set up by Steenway Productions.'

'Oh really. I'll take it. Check the dates.'

'Your diary's not exactly crowded, is it?'

'Money good?'

'Goodish. I'll ask for double.'

'Good lad. Thanks for that.'

'My pleasure. If I don't do things for you, you're clearly not going to do anything for yourself.'

'Cheerio, Maurice. Keep smiling.'

'What, with my worries? Cheerio.'

Work, too. And dressing-up. Charles was beginning to feel unaccountably cheerful. He rather relished the idea of secret investigations. With a jaunty step he went upstairs to his room to continue making-up.

Disguise is a matter of presenting oneself to the person deceived in an unexpected context. Then come tricks of stance and movement. Actual changing of colouring and features are less important. And Charles was quite pleased with his disguise. Certainly Joanne Menzies appeared not to recognise him, although he'd rather regretted choosing the character of Detective-Sergeant McWhirter of Scotland Yard when she revealed that she'd been brought up near the Kyles of Bute. But she seemed to accept the Glaswegian accent and his story of having left Scotland for London in his teens.

He had phoned her at Milton Buildings, saying that he had a routine enquiry to make about the Datsun, would have asked for Mr Marius Steen but, owing to the recent regrettable happening, wondered if she could help. She was efficiently affable, and invited him to come round straight away. So there he was, on the Friday morning, sitting opposite her, in the same chair that, only a week before, Charles Paris had occupied.

Detective-Sergeant McWhirter wore a nondescript brown and green suit, a Marks and Spencer pale yellow shirt and brown knitted tie. His shoes were stout brown brogues, suitable for the tramping from place to place which takes up most of a detective's time. When he entered the room he had hung up a pale mackintosh and a trilby hat. His hair was dark brown and slicked back with Brylcreem. He had thick horn-rimmed glasses, a heavy shadow and rather bad teeth. On his wedding finger was a worn gold band. He was the sort of man nobody would look at twice. No doubt a conscientious worker; no doubt a good husband and father; but totally unremarkable.

Miss Menzies couldn't be very helpful about the Datsun, though she answered all his questions very readily. Detective-Sergeant McWhirter explained that he was investigating a robbery in Pangbourne on Saturday night. An eye-witness claimed to have seen a yellow Datsun in the area at the relevant time, and McWhirter was painstakingly investigating all of the local Datsun-owners. The local police had told him that Mr Steen possessed such a vehicle, and he was just making a routine check on the whereabouts of the car at that time.

Miss Menzies felt certain it was in the garage at Mr Steen's Orme Gardens house all over the weekend.

When Mr Steen rang on Friday afternoon to say he wasn't certain whether or not he was returning to London at the weekend, she had checked the petrol in the car in case he might want it.

'This was Mr Marius Steen who rang?'

'No. This was his son Nigel. He rang to say that he was coming up to town that evening . . .'

'The Friday?'

'Yes. But that his father was still deep in his scripts, and wasn't sure of his movements. So I thought I'd better get some petrol in case Mr Marius Steen did come up to town over the weekend. You know what it's like getting petrol at the moment.'

Detective-Sergeant McWhirter nodded sagely, imagining his eleven-year-old Morris Traveller and the increasing difficulties of driving the wife and kids around. The foam rubber pads in Charles Paris's cheeks were beginning to feel acutely uncomfortable.

'I was lucky,' Miss Menzies continued. 'I managed to get a full tank. It's the garage I always go to.'

'And the tank still registered full on the Monday?'

'Yes.'

'And it wouldn't have done that if it had been driven down to Streatley and back?'

'Good heavens, no.' Miss Menzies looked at him as if he was mad.

'I'm sorry,' said Detective-Sergeant McWhirter stolidly. 'I do have to check all the details. Some cars have a petrol gauge that stays on full for a long time. If it's not properly adjusted.'

'Yes, of course. I'm sorry. The Datsun's does actually. It stays on "full" for quite a while and then drops rather fast.'

'But it wouldn't stay on full all the way to Streatley and back?'

'No. It's pretty good on petrol, but not that good.

Might just about make it one way without registering, but certainly not both. Anyway, nobody could have got into the garage at Orme Gardens. It's always locked.'

'Of course. Sorry about all this. We have to check. I'm afraid a detective's life is mostly spent chasing up blind alleys and wasting people's time.'

'That's quite all right.'

'Good.' Detective-Sergeant McWhirter rose to leave and then paused. 'That was very good of you, to look after the petrol. Part of your normal secretarial duties?'

'I am more of a personal assistant to Mr Steen than a secretary. I mean, I was.'

There was just a slight chink in her armour and he pressed a little further. 'Yes. A sad loss.'

'Yes.' He noticed how strained she was looking, much older than a week before. Though she was still immaculately groomed, there seemed somehow less poise about her, as if appearances remained, but the will had gone.

'So I suppose it's all up to the son now.'

'I suppose so.' She couldn't disguise the contempt she felt.

'Always sad for the family, this sort of thing. Is his wife still . . . er . . . ?'

'She died years ago.'

'Ah. And he never thought of remarrying?'

'No, he didn't.' She pronounced the words with sudden emphasis, and Charles saw clearly the situation which Jacqui's words—'She liked Marius'—had hinted at. Joanne Menzies had loved Marius Steen. Whether the love had ever been reciprocated or consummated he didn't know—though Steen's reputation made it likely—but the new fact opened interesting avenues of thought. She loved Steen, and she was passionately against his remarriage. The controlled force of her emotion when speaking of it had been frightening. A woman with feelings of that intensity might be capable of any action if she thought the man she loved was seriously in love with someone else. It added a new dimension to the picture.

CHAPTER TWELVE

THE UGLY SISTERS

When Charles got back to Hereford Road, there was a Swedish scrawl on the note pad—JERRY VENERAL RING. After a few moments' deciphering he rang Gerald Venables's number.

'Charles, look, we can't talk on the phone.' Gerald was obviously taking all the detective bit to heart, and entering into it with the spirit of a child's game of Cops and Robbers. 'Listen, I've found out about the "you-know-what." We must meet somewhere and talk.'

'OK. Where and when?'

'Two o'clock. The back bar of the Red Lion in Waverton Street.'

'Why? Is it quiet there?'

'No, but you can be overheard in quiet places. The Red Lion's so noisy, nobody'll hear a word,' said Gerald with complete seriousness.

'All right, Peewit.'

'What do you mean—Peewit?'

'Code-name. I'll be wearing a carnation. What's the password?' Charles put the phone down, imagining the expression on Gerald's face.

He was out of costume and looked like Charles Paris when he arrived in the back bar of the Red Lion. Squeezing past the milling lunchtime crowds he found himself pressed closely between Gerald and a rather busty Australian. 'Who's she?' he hissed.

'No idea. Where's your carnation?'

'That was a joke.'

'Oh.' Gerald sounded genuinely disappointed.

'Well, you recognise me, don't you?' Gerald was forced to admit he did. 'So, what gives?' Charles shouted above the din.

'Ssh.'

'What gives?' Softer.

'I beg your pardon.'

'Oh, for God's sake.'

Eventually, as the lunchtime crowds subsided office-wards and the pub was left to a few loud tourists, they found a quiet corner and sat down with their drinks. Charles had a pint and Gerald a dry martini (Charles almost expected him to ask for it 'shaken not stirred'). The solicitor looked round with conspicuous caution.

'The will is very interesting,' he hissed. 'Well, not so much the will as the whole situation. Basically, Nigel gets everything, but he's got a lot of it already.

'Marius Steen made over his three houses and about 75 per cent of his other assets to his son some years ago. You know, the old gift *inter vivos* dodge, to avoid estate duty.'

'I'm sorry. I don't know the old gift *inter vivos* dodge. I'm very stupid about the law.'

'So's everyone. That's what lawyers thrive on. What it basically means is that if someone makes a gift during his lifetime and doesn't die for a given period, that gift is free of estate duty, or partly free. There's a sliding scale. If the donor dies more than seven years after the gift, there's no duty at all payable. If he dies in the seventh year the whole duty is reduced by 60 per cent, if in the sixth by 30 per cent, and in the fifth 15 per cent.' Gerald was talking very fast and fluently, as he always did on the subject of money, but Charles reckoned he had got the gist. 'When was the gift made, Gerald?'

'Nearly six years ago.'

'So Nigel had absolutely no motive to kill his father. In fact, it was in his interests that the old man stayed alive.'

'Ah. That's it, is it?' Gerald's eyes narrowed in the manner of a thousand television thrillers. 'I think you'd better tell me the whole story, Charles.'

So he got the whole story, and when it was spelled out, the catalogue of suspicions and circumstantial evidence did sound pretty feeble. Gerald was clearly disappointed. 'That all hinges on Nigel Steen having a financial motive to kill his father, and, as you just observed, he very positively didn't have such a motive.'

'And it wouldn't have made any difference even if Marius Steen remarried?'

'It would have made a difference in the disposition of that part of the estate which hadn't been given away. But the gift of the rest couldn't be revoked. He had given away all rights in the property. You know, the freeholds were made over by deeds of gift by way of conveyance, and the—'

'Please talk English.'

'All right. Basically, all of the property is Nigel's—exclusively. Marius could not have any beneficial interest in any part of it. In other words, he couldn't benefit from the property or the dividends on the shares, or any part of the gift.'

'So what did he live on?'

'Interest from the remaining shares. Still quite a substantial amount, but only a tiny part of the whole.'

'And how could he still live in the houses?'

'He actually paid rent.'

'So if Nigel had wanted to, he could have turfed his father out of his own houses.'

'Yes. Because they weren't his own houses. They were Nigel's.'

'And what about the business? He still seemed in charge there.'

'Only in an advisory capacity. He made no profit from any of it.'

'Good God. So there again Nigel could have ousted him.'

'Could have done, but wasn't daft. He knew the business depended completely on his father's skill and instinct. No, Steen had organised it all very meticulously to avoid death duties. Nigel has been an incredibly wealthy young man for years.'

'How wealthy?'

'Certainly worth more than a million.'

'Shit.' Charles was impressed. 'And if none of this had been done what sort of death duties would have been charged?'

'80 per cent.'

'Blimey. The Government gets its pound of flesh, doesn't it. But Steen didn't go the full seven years.'

'No, he died just before the six came up. So estate duty is only going to be reduced by 30 per cent. Makes a nasty hole in Nigel's assumed possessions.'

'And certainly rules out any motive for murder.'

'Yes. The only motive for killing Marius Steen could be sheer bloody-mindedness on somebody's part—a desire to make things really difficult for Nigel. Is there anyone around who hates him that much?'

Though everyone seemed to despise Nigel, Charles hadn't met anyone whose feeling seemed strong enough to amount to hatred. It was Marius Steen who inspired violent emotions, not his son. 'And there's no mention of any legacy to Jacqui in the will?'

'None at all.'

'Hmm. I wonder what Marius Steen's letter meant.'

Charles felt depressed as he walked through Soho to Archer Street that evening. For a start there was the gloomy news he had to pass on to Jacqui. And then London itself was depressing. It was cold and dark.

Display lighting was out, as Edward Heath began his schoolmasterish campaign of mass deprivation, keeping the whole country in until the miners owned up that they were in the wrong. Time would show that the campaign had misjudged the reactions of the British public. Shops were dark, cold and uninviting. Familiar landmarks, like the neons of theatres and cinemas, disappeared. It was like the blackout, which Charles could suddenly remember with great clarity. A fifteen-year-old in grey flannel wandering around London in school holidays with an adolescent's apocalyptic vision, praying that he would lose his virginity before the bombs came and blasted him to oblivion.

He took a couple of wrong turnings in the gloom and was angry when he reached Jacqui's flat. He prepared an account of the will situation to break to her brutally. There was no point in kid gloves; she had to know sooner or later.

But he didn't get the chance to drop his thunderbolt. Jacqui opened the door in a state of high excitement, more colour and animation in her face than he had seen since the Steen affair started. 'Charles, come in. Bartlemas and O'Rourke are here!'

William Bartlemas and Kevin O'Rourke were a legend in the world of British Theatre. They were a middle-aged couple, whose main activity was the collection of memorabilia of the two great actors, Edmund Kean and William Macready. Bartlemas had an enormous private income, and the pair of them lived in a tall Victorian house in Islington, which was filled to the brim with playbills, prints, prompt copies, figurines and other souvenirs of their two heroes. They identified with them totally. Bartlemas was Kean, and O'Rourke Macready. In theory they were writing a book on the actors, but long since the fascination of collection for its own sake had taken over and work on the collation of evidence ceased. They spent all their time travelling round the British Isles, visiting auctions and antique shops, following hints and rumours, searching for more and more relics of their idols. But they always rushed back to London for the first night of every West End show. It was a point of honour that, if they were in the country, they'd be there, sitting in the middle of the fifth row of the stalls, both resplendent in Victorian evening dress, clutching shiny top hats and silver-topped canes. Quite what their role in British theatre was, was hard to define, but they knew everyone, everyone knew them and managements even came to regard their presence on a first night as an essential good luck charm. In the camper and more superstitious regions of the theatre world you'd often hear the sentence, 'My dear, Bartlemas and O'Rourke weren't there. The notices'll be up within the week.'

In appearance they fell rather short of their ideals. William Bartlemas was not tall, probably only about five foot seven, but his angular body gave the illusion of height and his knobbly limbs moved with adolescent awkwardness. His head was crowned with an astonished crest of dyed hair. It had that brittle crinkly texture born of much hairdressing, and was ginger, of a brightness to which nature has always been too shy to aspire. Kevin O'Rourke was tiny, with the pugnacious stance of a jockey and all the aggression of a butterfly. He was balding, and had countered the problem by combing what remained forward in a Royal Shakespeare Company Roman Plays style. The dyed black hair was as tight as skin over his head, except at the front where there was a curly fringe like the edge of a piecrust. The two always dressed identically—a grotesque pair of Beverley sisters. Today they were in oyster grey velvet. Meeting Bartlemas and O'Rourke was an unforgettable experience, and a fairly exhausting one. They talked non-stop in an elaborate relay race, one picking up the thread as soon as the other paused for breath.

They were delighted to see Charles. He had only met them once briefly at a party, but they remembered him effusively. 'Charles Paris,' said Bartlemas, 'lovely to see you. Haven't talked since that marvellous Bassanio you did at the Vic'—that had been fifteen years before—'lovely performance.'

'Yes,' said O'Rourke, 'you always were such a clever actor . . .'

'Sensational,' said Bartlemas. 'What are you up to now? My dear, we've just been on the most shattering binge in North Africa.'

'For months and months and months . . .'

'In Morocco, of course. O'Rourke disgraced himself continually. So much to drink, my dear, it wasn't true . . .'

'And Bartlemas almost got arrested more than once . . .'

'Oh, I didn't. Not really . . .'

'You did, dear, you did. I saw it all. This Moroccan policeman was watching you with a distinctly beady eye. And I don't think it was your perfection of form that intrigued him . . .'

'Well, be that as it may. We go off, we leave the collection and everything, miss all those divine first nights, just simply to have a holiday, to get away from everything . . .'

'But everything . . .'

'And we come back to hear this shattering news about Marius. Oh, it's too sad.'

'Too sad. We were just telling Jacqui here, we are absolutely desolated . . .'

'I mean he was so strong. And such a chum too . . .'

'I don't know how we'll survive without him, I really don't.'

'It's terrifying. If someone like Marius who was so robust . . .'

'So full of living . . .'

'If he can just pop off like that . . .'

'Then what chance is there for the rest of us?'

They both sat back, momentarily exhausted. Charles opened his mouth to speak, but missed the chance. 'So of course,' said Bartlemas, 'as soon as we heard the ghastly news about Marius, we just had to rush round here . . .'

'Immediately,' said O'Rourke. 'Because of *our secret.*'

They paused dramatically and gave Jacqui time to say, 'Charles, they've got a new will. Marius made another will.'

Charles looked round at Bartlemas and O'Rourke. They were glowing with importance. 'Yes,' said Bartlemas, 'we witnessed the will and he gave it to us to look after it . . .'

'Which is a pity,' said O'Rourke, 'because that means we can't inherit anything . . .'

'Not that he had anything we'd really like to inherit. I mean, nothing to do with Edmund and William . . .'

'No, but it would have been nice to have a little memento, wouldn't it, Bartlemas?'

'Oh yes. Yes, it would. You see, what happened was, we were in the South of France in the summer, when Jacqui and Marius were out there . . .'

'At Sainte-Maxime . . .'

'Yes. Marius's villa. Lovely spot . . .'

'Oh, lovely . . .'

'And suddenly, one night, after Jacqui had gone to bed, Marius suddenly said he was going to make a new will, and there was someone on holiday down there who was a solicitor—'

'Not his usual one?' Charles managed to slip in.

'Oh no, not dear Harold,' said Bartlemas.

'No, not Harold,' echoed O'Rourke. 'This was a rather sweet young man Marius found in a casino . . .'

'And anyway, Marius said this boy was coming over and he was going to draw up a new will, and would we witness it? . . .'

'So of course we said yes . . .'

'Well, we were so *intrigued*. It was so *exciting* . . .'

'And we've got it with us, and we were just about to show it to Jacqui when you arrived.'

'Look,' said Bartlemas, and, with a flourish, produced a sealed envelope from his inside pocket. At this gesture both he and O'Rourke burst out into riotous giggles. 'I'm sorry,' said O'Rourke when they had calmed down, 'it's just that that was the gesture Edmund Kean is supposed to have used on the "Is this a dagger?" speech in *Macbeth* at the New Theatre Royal, Drury Lane, in 1823.'

'Oh,' said Charles, as Bartlemas and O'Rourke went into new paroxysms of laughter. Again it took a little while for them to calm down and when they had, Bartlemas, with mock solemnity, handed the envelope to Jacqui. 'Of course,' he said conspiratorially, 'we know what's in it, don't we, O'Rourke?'

'Oh yes, Bartlemas.' They both sat back with smug smiles on their faces and looked at Jacqui, like favourite uncles watching a child unwrap their Christmas present.

Jacqui opened the envelope, pulled out a document and looked at the sheet for some long time. Then she looked up, perplexed. 'It's all in funny English.'

'That's because it's a legal document,' said Charles. 'They are always incomprehensible. It's a point of honour among lawyers never to be understood.'

'You read it, and tell me what it means.' Jacqui handed the document over.

'We could tell you what's in it,' said Bartlemas.

'Yes, but we won't,' said O'Rourke coyly.
Charles read the will.

I, MARIUS LADISLAS STENIATOWSKI, commonly known as MARIUS STEEN, and hereinafter referred to as such, of 173, Orme Gardens, London, W2 and 'Rivalon,' Streatley-on-Thames in the County of Berkshire, Theatrical Impresario, HEREBY REVOKE all wills and testamentary documents heretofore made by me AND DECLARE this to be my LAST WILL

1. I APPOINT WILLIAM DOUGLAS D'ABERNON BARTLEMAS and KEVIN CORNELIUS O'ROURKE to be jointly the Executors of this my WILL.

2. In the event of my dying before remarriage, I DEVISE and BEQUEATH all of my real and personal estate whatsoever and wheresoever not already disposed of as to my freeholds in fee simple and as to my personal estate absolutely to the issue of my union with JACQUELINE MYRTLE MITCHELL, the property to be held in trust for the said issue, the trust allowing a monthly sum of not less than FIVE HUNDRED POUNDS to the said JACQUELINE MYRTLE MITCHELL to pay for the upbringing of the said issue, this arrangement to cease on his or her attaining the age of twenty-one years, whereupon a quarter of the remaining estate—whether in freehold property, stocks, shares or chattels shall be granted in perpetuity to the said JACQUELINE MYRTLE MITCHELL, and the remainder to be granted to the said issue. In the event of the said JACQUELINE MYRTLE MITCHELL dying before the child attains twenty-one years, all of the estate shall devolve upon the said child and be held for him or her in trust, as my executors and their appointees shall advise.

IN WITNESS whereof I the said MARIUS STEEN the Testator have to this my LAST WILL set my hand this fifteenth day of October One Thousand Nine Hundred and Seventy-Three.

SIGNED AND ACKNOWLEDGED by the abovenamed MARIUS STEEN the Testator as and for his LAST WILL in the presence of us both present at the same time who at his request in his presence and in the presence of each other have hereunto subscribed our names as witnesses:

William Bartlemas
17, Ideal Road,
Islington
Keanophile
Kevin O'Rourke
17, Ideal Road
Islington
Macreadophile

Jacqui was looking at him eagerly. Obviously she had understood the gist of the will and just wanted confirmation. Charles grinned. 'Basically you'll be all right. You can afford to have that baby.'

'What, and the baby'll get everything?'

'Not exactly, no.' And Charles explained briefly about the gift *inter vivos* to Nigel. 'So what we're talking about is only 25 per cent of Marius Steen's assets other than the houses. Mind you, it's still more money than you've ever seen in your life.'

Bartlemas and O'Rourke had been silent too long and burst again into stereo action.

'Ooh,' said Bartlemas, 'fancy all that going to little Arsehole . . .'

'Who?'

'Nigel,' said O'Rourke patronisingly. 'Everyone calls him little Arsehole. Why on earth would Marius make all that over to him?'

'It's the family thing, isn't it,' said Bartlemas. 'Marius always wanted to found a dynasty.'

'But I thought he and Nigel didn't get on.' Charles was still rather puzzled by the whole gift business.

'Well, it varied, didn't it, O'Rourke?'

'Oh yes, up and down all the time . . .'

'I remember, there was a time when Nigel ran off to America . . .'

'With some woman, ghastly actress . . .'

'But ghastly. Marius was awfully upset. Nigel stayed away for two, three years . . .'

'All of that, Bartlemas, all of that. Then he came crawling back . . .'

'Tail between his legs. Woman had left him . . .'

'Who could blame her? Marius really did the prodigal son bit . . .'

'Oh yes, you couldn't move in Orme Gardens for fatted calf. All the great reconciliation, my son, my son . . .'

'It's the Jewish character, you know. Love of the family. Terribly important to them . . .'

'You're right, O'Rourke. That's what it is.' This was pronounced with finality and followed by a breath pause. Charles, who was beginning to understand the technique of conversation with Bartlemas and O'Rourke, leapt in. 'When was it this reconciliation took place?'

'About five or six years ago,' said Bartlemas.

'Ah, that figures. It must have been then, in a final flush of family feeling, that he made everything over to Nigel.'

'Yes.'

'And, so far as one can tell, he regretted it ever after.'

'Yes,' said O'Rourke. There was a pause. 'Jacqui,' said Charles. 'I didn't know your middle name was Myrtle.'

'It was after an aunt,' said Jacqui.

CHAPTER THIRTEEN

WHO DOES THE SLIPPER FIT?

The new will was passed over to Gerald Venables, who got in touch with Harold Cohn of Cohn, Jarvis, Cohn and Stickley, and the law began the grindingly slow processes on which it thrives. Charles thought that the whole affair was now out of his hands, and, though it was unsatisfactory that so many questions remained unanswered, at least some kind of justice had been done. Nigel got most of the estate, but would be more than a little embarrassed by estate duty; and provision for Jacqui and her baby would be sorted out in time. If the police persevered, they were bound to crack Audrey Sweet's defence and find out about the family blackmailing business. Then they had only to check through the photographs and the Sally Nash guest lists (which, as the case at the Old Bailey trickled on inexorably, were becoming public property anyway) to find their murderer. Charles even felt a twinge of pity for Mrs Sweet. She was a desperate woman, her incompetent attempts at blackmail motivated only by a desire to get as much money as possible in her new widowhood. It was now three days since Bill Holroyd had promised to bring her ten thousand pounds and by now she must realise the likelihood of his appearance was decreasing.

It was Saturday 15th December. Christmas was coming, but without much conviction in a darkened Britain. The cold shops with their sad gas-lamps were full of Christmas shoppers feeling sorry for themselves, and shoplifters having a field day. The ever-present possibility of bombs made buying presents even jollier.

Charles rose late and managed to beat one of the Swedes into the bathroom. He returned to his room wrapped cosily in his towelling dressing-gown and sat in front of the gas-fire with a cup of coffee. Now that the excitements of the last fortnight were over, he would have to think again about getting some work. True, he'd got *The Zombie Walks* coming up, but that wasn't going to make him a millionaire, and the old overdraft was getting rather overblown. Perhaps the answer was to write another television play. But, even if he could write the thing quickly, all the subsequent processes took such a bloody long time. Getting the thing accepted, rewritten, rewritten, rewritten, rehearsed, recorded, edited, scheduled, rescheduled, rescheduled, rescheduled ad infinitum. Not much likelihood of getting a commission either. Charles Paris wasn't a big enough name these days. And no doubt, with the prospects of a three-day week and early closedown, none of the television companies would commit themselves to anything.

But as he tried to think of his work (Charles had long since ceased to grace it with the name of 'his career'), his thoughts kept returning to the Steen situation. There was something fishy about the whole set-up. He tried to think himself into a detective frame of mind. What would Sherlock Holmes do in the circumstances? He would sit puffing on his pipe, Dr Watson goggle-eyed with admiration at his side, and suddenly, by a simple process of deduction, arrive at the complete solution. Somehow Charles Paris, sitting on his own in a towelling dressing-gown, hadn't quite the same charisma. Or the same powers of deduction.

Reflecting sadly on his inadequacy, Charles rose to get dressed. He opened the dull grey wardrobe and pulled a pair of trousers off a hanger. As he did so, he noticed that there was a dark smudge on the seat. It smelled of petrol. He was about to put his trousers back and take out another pair, when a sudden thought stopped him in his tracks.

The trousers he was holding were the ones he'd been wearing at Streatley the previous weekend. And he must have got the mark on them when he slipped over in Steen's garage. The scene came back to him with immediate clarity of detail. The enormous bulk of the blue Rolls illuminated by his torch, then suddenly his feet going from under him, slipping in a pool of petrol, landing on a spanner and a piece of tubing.

A piece of tubing. And the Rolls petrol gauge registered empty. Joanne Menzies' words about the Datsun came back to him—'It's pretty good on petrol, but not that good. Might just about make it one way without registering, but certainly not both.' But what was simpler than to drive the car to Streatley, siphon petrol out of the Rolls into it (possibly even siphon some into a can as well, to top it up near London) and then drive back? Charles decided that a visit should be paid to Mr Nigel Steen.

Joanne Menzies still looked drawn and strained when she ushered Detective-Sergeant McWhirter into Mr Steen's office on the Monday afternoon. The policeman thanked her and stood deferentially until he was invited to sit down.

The man who made the invitation was very like his father, but without the vitality that had distinguished Marius Steen. Nigel had the same beak of a nose, but, without the dark eyes, its effect was comic rather than forceful. His eyes were blue, a legacy from the English rose whom Marius had married; and his hair was light brown rather than the black which his father had kept, only peppered with grey, until his death. The general effect was of a diluted Marius Steen, ineffectual and slightly afraid.

Nigel was ostentatiously smoking a big cigar to give an illusion of poise. He flashed Charles what was meant to be a frank smile. 'Well, what can I do to help?'

'I'm very sorry to bother you,' said Detective-Inspector McWhirter slowly, 'and I do very much appreciate your putting yourself out to see me. Particularly at what must be a very distressing time for you.'

'That's quite all right. What is it?' With a hint of irritation, or was it anxiety?

'I have already spoken to your secretary on the matter and she proved most helpful.' Charles reiterated his lies about the theft in Pangbourne on the Saturday night.

'But you see, since I spoke to her, we have had another witness's account of having seen a yellow Datsun in the Goring area. And they identified your number plate. I mean, you can never trust members of the public; they are extraordinarily inaccurate in what they claim to remember, but I can't discount anything. All I'm trying to do is to establish where your father's Datsun was on that night, and then stop wasting your time.'

'Yes.' Nigel drew on the cigar and coughed slightly. He was clearly rattled. Not a man with a strong nerve, and certainly on the surface not one who could carry out a cold-blooded murder. He capitulated very quickly. 'As a matter of fact, I was in Streatley in the Datsun on that Saturday night.'

Charles felt a great surge of excitement, but Detective-Sergeant McWhirter only said, 'Ah.'

'Yes. I'd phoned my father in the evening, and he didn't sound too well, so I drove down to see how he was.'

'And how was he?'

'Fine, fine. We had a few drinks together, chatted. He seemed in very good form. Then I drove back to London.'

'Still on the Saturday night?'

'Yes. It's not far.'

'No, no, of course not.' Charles was about to ask about the subterfuge of the full petrol tank, but decided that Detective-Sergeant McWhirter might not be in possession of all the relevant facts for that deduction. As it happened, Nigel continued defensively without needing further questions.

'You're probably wondering why I didn't mention this fact before. Well, to tell you the truth, your boys asked me when had I last seen my father alive and I said Friday instinctively, and then by the time I'd realised my mistake, it was all written down, and, you know, I thought if I changed it, that'd only create trouble.'

It sounded pretty implausible to Charles, but Detective-Sergeant McWhirter gave a reassuring nod. 'Yes, of course, sir. And you're quite sure that while the car was down in Streatley, the thieves who I'm after wouldn't have had a chance to take it and use it for their break-in?'

'No, that would be quite impossible. I put the car in the garage and I'm sure I'd have heard it being driven off. Anyway, I wasn't down there very long.'

'No. Oh well, fine, Mr Steen. Thank you very much.' Detective-Sergeant McWhirter rose to leave. 'I think I'd better start looking for another yellow Datsun.'

'Yes. And . . . er . . . Detective-Sergeant . . .'

'Yes?'

'Will you have to mention the discrepancy in my story—you know, my confusion about when I last saw my father—?'

'Good Lord, no. That's quite an understandable mistake in a moment of emotion, sir. So long as an account's written down somewhere, no one's going to fuss about the details. After all, there wasn't anything unusual about your father's death. If there had been any grounds for suspicion, it'd be a different case.' And Detective-Sergeant McWhirter laughed.

Nigel Steen laughed too, Charles thought a bit too heartily. But perhaps he was being hypersensitive and letting his suspicions race like Jacqui's.

'Anyway,' the Detective-Sergeant continued, 'I don't have anything to do with your father's death. Different department, you know.'

'Yes, of course.'

'Well, goodbye, Mr Steen. And thank you again for your help. If only more members of the public were as cooperative as you have been, our life would be a lot easier.'

They shook hands. Nigel's felt like a damp facecloth. Detective-Sergeant McWhirter went through into Miss Menzies's anteroom. 'All sorted out now?' she asked brightly.

'Yes, thank you, Miss Menzies.'

'Hmm. We've seen quite a lot of you lately.'

'Yes,' said the Detective-Sergeant casually, unprepared for what happened next.

Miss Menzies suddenly stood up, looked him straight in the eyes and said, 'Do you know it's a very serious offence to impersonate a police officer?'

'Yes,' said Detective-Sergeant McWhirter slowly, waiting to see what came next.

'I rang up Scotland Yard to tell you something this morning, and they'd never heard of you.'

'Ah.'

'And from the start I thought your accent was a bit phoney. I know a lot of people who come from Glasgow.'

'Yes.' There was a pause. Then Charles continued, still in his discredited Glaswegian. 'Well, what was it you rang up the Yard to tell me?'

Joanne Menzies looked at him coolly. 'You've got a

nerve. But I think you're probably doing something I'd sympathise with, so I'll tell you. I checked with Morrison, the chauffeur at Orme Gardens, and he was suspicious that the Datsun may have been used on the Saturday night.'

'Yes, I know. I've just got that from Mr Nigel Steen.'

'Ah.' She sounded disappointed that her information was redundant. 'You're suspicious of him too, aren't you?'

'Maybe.'

'No maybe,' she said, 'you are. Incidentally, "Detective-Sergeant," what's your real name?'

'Charles Paris.'

'Ah.' Her eyes widened and she nodded slowly. 'Very good.' It was a warming compliment, from someone who knew about the theatre. 'Well, Charles, if there's anything else I can tell you, or I can find out for you, let me know.'

'Thanks.' As he was leaving, he turned and looked at her. 'You hate Nigel Steen, don't you?'

'Yes,' she said simply.

Christmas intervened and the business of investigation was suspended. Charles told Jacqui the new information he'd gleaned, but met with little luck in following it up. When he rang Joanne to check Nigel's movements in the week before Steen's death, a strange female voice answered and informed him that Miss Menzies had already gone up to Scotland for her Christmas holidays. Gerald Venables was getting a very slow response from Cohn, Jarvis, Cohn and Stickley on the matter of the new will, and also seemed preoccupied with family arrangements and Christmas drink parties. His enthusiasm for the cloak-and-dagger business of detection seemed to have waned.

Charles felt his own sense of urgency ebbing too.

Though he got excited at each new development in his investigations, he soon became disillusioned again. And Joanne's seeing through his disguise made him a bit wary. He had no particular desire to break the law. Detection was a serious business, and perhaps he should leave it alone. The days of the gifted amateur investigator were over. It was better to leave everything to the police, who with superior training and equipment must stand a greater chance of uncovering crime.

And each time Charles looked at his progress it seemed more negative. Though he had enjoyed his little investigations and masquerades, his only real discovery was that Nigel Steen had tried to disguise the fact of driving down to Streatley on the night of Saturday 8th December. And though the visit could have given him an opportunity to kill his father, and then drive down the next day to discover the body, that was the one crime which every logical motive screamed against. By killing Marius then, Nigel would have been sacrificing a great deal of money. Duties at 80 per cent on an estate of a million, only reduced by 30 per cent, because of the donor's death before the end of the sixth year (to borrow Gerald Venables's terminology) would mean that Nigel would be paying more than half a million in estate duty. Whereas if he only waited till the seven years were up, all the given property would be his without any tax. It's a rare character who commits murder in order to lose a million pounds.

And the only other fact, hanging around in the background, was Bill Sweet's death, which, by some fairly dubious reasoning and some circumstantial evidence, could be laid at Marius Steen's door. But Marius Steen was dead. Why bother him now?

The Montrose was open over Christmas and so, along with a lot of other divorced and debauched actors, Charles Paris spent a week sublimely pissed.

* * *

He was feeling distinctly drink-sodden when the phone rang on the morning of the 3rd of January, 1974. He wanted to be picked up and wrung out like a floor cloth to get the stuff out of his system. He lay in bed, hoping the phone would go away or someone would answer it. But the Swedish girls were still in Sweden for the holidays and he was alone in the house. The phone went on ringing.

He stumped savagely downstairs and picked up the receiver. 'Hello.' His voice came out as a croak.

'It's Jacqui.' Her voice was excited again, bubbling. 'Charles, I've been to the police.'

'What?'

'About Nigel. I went to Scotland Yard this morning and saw an Inspector and told him all about our suspicions, and about how we knew Nigel had been down at Streatley that Saturday—'

'I hope you didn't tell him how we found out.'

'No, I didn't. I didn't mention you at all.'

'Thank God for that.'

'Anyway, the Inspector said it all sounded very suspicious and he's going to authorise an aupopsy—'

'Autopsy.'

'Yes. Anyway, he's getting an order to have Marius exhumed and check the cause of death. He took everything I said very seriously.' The last sentence was pronounced with pride. There was a pause; she was waiting for him to react. 'Well, what do you think, Charles?'

'I don't know. In a way, I think it's asking for trouble . . .'

'Oh, Charles, we've got to know whether or not Marius was murdered.'

'Have we? It's all sorted out. The baby's being looked after . . .'

'Charles, do you mean that?'

'No.'

'We've got to know.'

'Yes. When's the exhumation to be?'

'Quite soon. Probably next Monday.'

'And when will the results be known?'

'End of next week. There should be an inquest on Friday.'

'You realise that, by doing this, you have virtually made a public accusation of murder against Nigel?'

'Yes. And that is exactly what I meant to do.'

Ten days passed. In America, with the tide of Watergate rising around him, President Nixon celebrated his sixty-first birthday. In England wild storms swept the country, and commuters were infuriated and inconvenienced by the ASLEF dispute. Housewives started panic buying of toilet rolls. And in a churchyard in Goring, the body of Marius Steen was moved from its grave after a stay of only four short weeks. Then it was opened up and samples of its organs were taken and analysed.

All of these events, international and domestic, seemed unreal to Charles. Since sobering up after Christmas he had degenerated into a deep depression. Inactivity and introspection left him lethargic and uninterested in anything. His usual solutions to the problem—drink and sex—were ineffectual. He drank heavily, but it gave him no elation, merely intensified his mood. And his self-despite was so strong that he knew reviving an old flame or chasing some young actress would only aggravate it. He tried to write, but couldn't concentrate. Instead he sat in his room, his mind detached, looking down on his body and despising what he saw. Forty-seven years old, creatively and emotionally sterile. He thought of going to see Frances, but didn't feel worthy of her warmth and eternal forgiveness. She had sent him four stout dependable Marks and Spencer shirts for Christmas, nursing him like a mother who respects her child's independence. He'd sent her Iris Murdoch's latest novel. In hardback, which he knew she'd think an unnecessary extravagance.

His only comfort was that the following Monday he was to start filming *The Zombie Walks*. Though he didn't view the prospect with any sort of enthusiasm (he'd been sent a script, but hadn't bothered to read it) he knew that activity of some sort, something he had to do, was always better than nothing. Eventually, if enough kept happening, the mood would lift without his noticing its departure and he would hardly remember the self-destructive self that went with it.

But as he walked through the dim streets of London to Archer Street on the Friday evening, the mood was still with him. He felt remote, viewing himself as a third person. And he had a sense of gloom about the findings of the inquest.

When Jacqui opened the door of her flat, he knew from her face that his forebodings had been justified. She was silent until he'd sat down. Then she handed him a glass of Southern Comfort and said, 'Well, that's that.'

'What?'

'According to the coroner, Marius died of natural causes.'

'A heart attack?'

'They had some fancy medical term for it, but yes, that's what they said.'

'Well.' Charles sighed. He couldn't think of anything else to say. Jacqui looked on the verge of tears, and, as usual, converted her emotion into a violent outburst. 'Little Arsehole's been clever, the sod. He must have given Marius an electric shock, or injected air into his veins, or—'

'Jacqui, you've been watching too much television. That sort of thing just doesn't happen. I'm afraid we have to accept the fact that Marius did die from natural causes, and that all our suspicions of Nigel have been slander, just based on dislike and nothing else.'

'No, I don't believe it.'

'Jacqui, you've got to believe it. There's nothing else you can do.'

'Well, why did he go down to Streatley on the Saturday night, and make such a bloody secret of it?'

'I don't know. Perhaps for the reasons he said. He was worried about his father, so he went down, they had a few drinks, then he came back to London.'

'Oh, for Christ's sake, that won't wash.'

'Why not?'

'He and Marius didn't get on at the time. We know that from the new will and the letter to me and—'

'Perhaps they had another reconciliation.'

'Piss off, Charles. There's something fishy and Nigel's behind it. Marius was murdered.'

'Jacqui, the most sophisticated forensic tests have proved that he wasn't.'

'Well, they're wrong. They're all bloody wrong. Nigel paid them off. He bribed them.'

'Now you're getting childish.'

'I am not getting bloody childish!' Jacqui stood up and looked as if she was about to hit him. Charles didn't respond and after a frozen pause, she collapsed into a chair and burst out crying. When he had calmed her, she announced very coolly. 'I'm not going to stop, Charles. I'll get him. From now on there's a war between Nigel and me.'

'Well, you certainly nailed your colours to the mast by setting up the post-mortem.'

'Yes. And I'm going to win.' Thereafter she didn't mention anything about either of the Steens for the rest of the evening. She cooked another of her frozen meals (country rissoles) and Charles drank moderately (a rather vinegary Spanish Rioja). Then they watched the television. She had just bought (in anticipation of her legacy) a new Sony portable ('I'll be sitting about a lot when I get very big'). There wasn't much on the box, but that night it was preferable to conversation. At ten-thirty, by Government orders, came the closedown. Charles rose and after a few mumbled words about thanks, and keeping in touch, and being cheerful, and seeing himself out, he left.

Jacqui's flat was on the top floor and the bulb in the light on her landing had long since gone and not been replaced. As Charles moved forward to the familiar step, he felt his ankle caught, and his body, overbalancing, hurtled forward down the flight of stairs.

The noise brought Jacqui to the door and light spilled out over the scene. 'Charles, are you all right? Are you drunk, or what?'

He slowly picked himself up. The flight was only about ten steps down to the next landing, and though he felt bruised all over, and shocked, nothing seemed to be broken. 'No, I'm not drunk. Look.'

And he pointed up to the top step. Muzzily outlined in the light was a wire, tied tightly between the banisters on either side. It was about four inches above the step. Jacqui turned pale, and let out a little gasp of horror. 'Good God. Were they trying to kill me?'

'No!' said Charles, as he leaned, aching, against the wall at the foot of the flight. Suddenly he realised the flaw in the will Marius Steen had so hastily improvised in the South of France. 'I don't think it was you they wanted to kill. Just your baby.'

CHAPTER FOURTEEN

SLAPSTICK SCENE

The Zombie Walks was one of the worst film scripts ever conceived. The Zombie (played by a well-known Horror Film Specialist) had walked for a thousand years in a subterranean cavern which was broken open by an earthquake in Lisbon. By means not specified, from Portugal he arrived in Victorian England, where he got the idea that Lady Laetitia Winthrop (played by a 'discovery' from the world of modelling, whose acting talent was 36-23-36) was his long-lost love from a world before the subterranean cavern. He therefore determined to seize her from Winthrop Grange where she lived with her father Lord Archibald Winthrop (played by a well-known character actor who did commercials for tea bags). After the Zombie's travels through Victorian London (where, incidentally, he committed the crimes attributed to Jack the Ripper) he arrived at the Grange and enlisted the help of Tick, a deformed coachman of evil character (played by Charles Paris). As the Zombie progressed, he committed murder after murder, and his victims, rather than dying and lying down, became zombies too, until at the end Winthrop Grange was besieged by a whole army of the walking dead. Had it not been for the activities of Lady Laetitia's lover, bold Sir Rupert Cartland (played by an odious young actor who'd risen to prominence by playing a tough naval lieutenant in a television series) making with the garlic and the wooden stakes (a bit of vampire lore crept into the script), Lady Laetitia and her father would have been turned into zombies and carried back to the subterranean cave, where they would never be heard of again. Which, to Charles's mind, wouldn't have been a bad thing.

They were filming at Bloomwater, a stately home in Berkshire which had been built by Sir Henry Manceville, an eccentric nobleman, in 1780. Manceville had designed it himself as a great Gothic palace and even incorporated the specially-built ruins of an abbey into one wing. It was a monumental folly, which could have been made for horror films. In fact, had the cinema been invented at the time, it probably would have been. Sir Henry Manceville had been obsessed with ghosts and, in later life, when his eccentricity slid into madness, he used to terrify his servants by walking the Long Gallery, dressed in a sheet, dragging a length of chain and wailing piteously.

Bloomwater's present owner was a more prosaic figure, Sir Lionel Newman, the paper magnate. He was a man who, like Marius Steen, had risen from humble origins to immense wealth and had surrounded himself with all the symbols of the established aristocracy. His association with Marius Steen had been the reason why Bloomwater was being used for the filming.

Charles found that, as ever, making a film involved much more hanging around than actual work. The director, a little Cockney who glorified in the name of Jean-Luc Roussel, generated an impression of enormous activity as he buzzed around checking camera angles, getting the lighting changed, demonstrating the special effects and bawling out the continuity girl. But very little actually seemed to get done.

Charles didn't find many sympathetic characters among the cast. The Horror Film Specialist was surrounded by an admiring coterie of lesser horror film specialists and most of their conversation referred back to previous triumphs. ('Do you remember that *Dracula* when your fang got stuck in the girl's bra?'; or 'I'll never forget that girl who had hysterics during that human sacrifice'; or 'Do you remember that take as the Werewolf when you forgot your line and said "Bow-Wow"?') They all sat around, reminding each other of things they all remembered, each waiting his cue for the next reminiscence to be slotted in.

So Charles went off on his own most of the time. He sat in the Library (later to be the scene of the appallingly-written quarrel between Lord Archibald and Sir Rupert) and did the crossword or played patience.

On the Wednesday morning of the first week of the schedule he was sitting with the cards spread before him and feeling fairly secure. The film world still has an outdated generosity in its dealings with actors. The big-spending Hollywood myth retains its influence and the Zombie cast were well looked after by Steenway Productions, with cars organised to get them to and from the set. The early starts were a disadvantage, but Charles had minimised that by staying with Miles and Juliet and having the car pick him up at six. Then he could sleep through the drive and the laborious business of make-up. Quite cosy. And the money was good.

He also felt as secure as he could about Jacqui. The shock of the trip-wire incident had worn off and she was fairly well hidden. He'd wanted to send her off to some relative in the country, but she didn't seem to have any family. In fact, when they went into it, it was amazing how few people Jacqui had to call on. No family, or at least none she kept in touch with, no girlfriends. The centre of her life had always been men, either one at a time or many. A lot of girls end up promiscuous, when all they're looking for is friendship. Jacqui's lack of other resources explained both her desolation when Steen seemed to have dropped her and her reliance on Charles. (Even her leaping into bed with him again. She needed to keep up her continuity of male companionship, and humbly thought she had nothing to offer but sex.)

Charles had considered parking her on Frances in Muswell Hill, but the incongruity of the thought of the two women together was too great. So in the end he had given her his keys to the room in Hereford Road. He felt fairly confident that Nigel Steen, or whoever was mounting the campaign against her, did not know of any tie-up with Charles Paris. Hereford Road was dangerously near Orme Gardens, but it was only a short-term solution while the film lasted. Jacqui was likely to stay in most of the time with her portable television; her pregnancy made her quite content to do so. Obviously she'd have to go out to the shops from time to time, but she'd had her hair dyed black on the Saturday, bought a new winter coat and a large pair of dark glasses. That should keep her safe. Charles could imagine Jacqui quite happy in her enforced confinement. Hers was not a demanding character, and so long as she felt some evidence of a man's care (which living in Charles's room would give her) she would not need more. When the Zombie had finished his walk, a more permanent method of protecting her for the next four months would have to be found.

They'd considered going to the police, but agreed that, after the embarrassing *débâcle* of the inquest, further accusations from Jacqui against Nigel Steen would sound more like the ramblings of a paranoid than anything else. It was safer for her simply to go underground. Charles rang daily to check everything was all right.

So he felt secure as he sat looking over the rolling lawns of Bloomwater. To add to his pleasure, the patience came out. He was just laying the cards down for another game, when he heard the door open behind him. He turned and the girl who had just come in let out a little scream.

For a moment he couldn't think what was worrying her, until he remembered his make-up. His own hair was hidden under a latex cap from which a few grey wisps straggled crazily. His eyes were red-rimmed and sagging, his nose a mass of pustules, and his teeth had been blacked out with enamel. The whole face had the unearthly green tinge of dead flesh, which Jean-Luc Roussel was convinced was the mark of a zombie.

'I'm sorry,' said Charles. 'I'm afraid I do look rather a fright.'

'Oh, that's all right. I just wasn't expecting it.' The girl looked about sixteen and recently aware of her considerable attractions. Her black hair was swept back in the careless style the only the most expensive hair-dressing can give. She was wearing check trousers and a red polo-necked sweater that accentuated the perfect roundness of her bra-less small breasts. For the first time in over a month Charles felt certain that he hadn't lost interest in sex.

'I take it you're in the film,' said the girl.

'No, I always look like this. You're making fun of my natural affliction.'

The girl was checked for a moment, then laughed. 'That's not fair. Who are you?'

'I am Tick, the deformed coachman,' he said in his First Witch voice ('Macabre in the extreme'—*Plays and Players*).

She laughed again. Obviously she was still at an age to be amused by funny voices. Charles felt distinctly inclined to show off. 'No, who are you really?' she asked.

'Charles Paris.'

'Oh, I think I've heard of you,' she said, polite but uncertain. 'Ooh, just a minute. Were you ever at the Royal Shakespeare Company at Stratford?'

'Yes, a long time ago.'

'About seven years?'

'Yes.'

'Did you play Cassius in *Julius Caesar*?'

'Yes.'

'Ooh. I thought you were marvellous. We went in a school trip. We all got quite silly about you.'

'Oh,' said Charles, in what stage directions describe as a self-deprecating manner. This was all rather playing into his hands. Seeds sown unknowingly long ago. Cast your bread upon the waters, and it will come back buttered. 'Who are you then?'

'I'm Felicity Newman. I live here. Daddy owns this place.' (The 'Daddy' caught the slight quack of an English girls' public school. It was a sound Charles had always found exciting.) 'I'm fascinated by all this filming. Somebody's going to show me round, a friend of Daddy's. I want to work in films.'

'With your looks I should think you'd stand a very good chance.'

'No, silly.' She was still sufficiently girlish to blush at the formula compliment. 'Not that side of films. The production side. I'm doing a secretarial course and want to get in that way. Daddy knows quite a lot of people in the cinema.'

Yes. Charles felt sure that Daddy could pull the odd string on his daughter's behalf. Sir Lionel Newman put a great deal of money into film production. Charles even had a feeling that he was a major shareholder in Steenway Productions. 'And how come you're not doing your secretarial course today?' he asked in the Morningside accent which he had drummed into the cast of his production of *The Prime of Miss Jean Brodie* ('Slow-moving'—*Evening Argus*).

She giggled. 'Oh, I just took the day off. How do you do that Scottish accent?'

She was easily impressed, but Charles felt like indulging himself in a little *tour de force*. He went through his entire gamut of the accents of Scotland, from his Hebridean fisherman through to the harsh tones of Glasgow. Indeed, he was in full flood in his Detective-Sergeant McWhirter voice, to an accompaniment of giggles from Felicity, when he heard a voice behind him. 'Ah, there you are.'

He stopped in mid-flow and turned to see Nigel Steen standing in the doorway. Steen looked annoyed, but it was difficult to tell whether or not he had recognised the voice. 'Felicity. I'm sorry to have kept you. Shall we start our tour?'

'Yes. Certainly, Nigel.' She was suddenly downcast, obviously sharing the world's lack of enthusiasm for Marius Steen's son. 'Do you know Charles Paris?' she asked.

'No, I don't think we've met,' said Nigel Steen, and he looked at Charles intently.

The scenes to be shot were rescheduled and Charles didn't in fact do anything that day. When this truth, which had been apparent from early morning, was finally recognised by Jean-Luc Roussel and Charles was released, it was about five o'clock. In a state of some exasperation, he was about to organise his car back to Pangbourne, when Felicity appeared round the corner of one of the make-up caravans. 'Hello,' she said brightly, 'do you fancy a drink?'

It was exactly what Charles did fancy (or at least part of what he fancied), so he said so. 'Come on,' said Felicity, and led him round the back of the house and through a herb-garden into a large modern kitchen. 'This is the part of the house we actually use. The rest's just for show.' She led him upstairs to a homely-looking sitting-room, and opened the drinks cupboard. 'What?'

'Scotch, please.'

She took out a bottle of Glenfiddich and poured a wine-glassful. 'Hey. Stop.'

'Why?'

'It's an expensive malt whisky.'

'I know,' she said superciliously, and passed him the glass. He took a long sip. It was very welcome. Felicity still looked rather piqued at his assumption of her ignorance of drink lore. He tried to open out the conversation. 'Still keen on films after seeing them in action for a day?'

'Yes,' she said shortly, and then, to show her sophistication in the matter of alcohol, 'I think I'll have a gin and tonic.'

'So it was a good day?' Charles knew he sounded horribly patronising.

'All right. The company could have been better.'

'Nigel Steen, the great impresario.'

'Shit,' she said unexpectedly. 'He's a creep, always has been. I've known him for years. Daddy knew Marius. I think they had plans for matchmaking. Yeugh.'

'Not your type?'

'God, no. I don't know what my type is really, but it's not that. Ergh. He made a pass at me once. It was horrible, like being groped by liver. Actually, he invited me out tonight, probably with an ulterior motive. I told him I was otherwise engaged.'

'Are you?'

'No. Not unless you'd like me to cook you a meal.'

'Oh well . . . I'm sure that you don't want—'

'It's no sweat. I'm doing this Cordon Bleu course as well as the secretarial thing, and I need the practice.'

So they both agreed to show off for the evening. She demonstrated her culinary skills with a splendid Chicken Kiev and Dauphinoise potatoes, and he kept her entertained with a variety of accents and theatrical reminiscences. Felicity raided her father's cellar for a couple of bottles of an excellent Château Margaux. 'He'll never notice. Doesn't know a thing about wine. Just takes advice all the time.'

'Where are your parents?'

'Oh, they've gone to Jamaica. As soon as all these lighting restrictions came in, Daddy said he wasn't going to stay in England and they pissed off.' Felicity's lapses into strong language, which were meant to make her sound cool, only made her sound immature. But appealing.

Charles found it very difficult. This girl was plainly throwing herself at him, and he knew that if he took advantage of something so easy, he would really feel shabby. And she looked sixteen. Possibly even under age. There is a point where going around with younger women stops and cradle-snatching begins. And Charles prided himself that he had never knowingly taken advantage of anyone (anyone, that is, who didn't deserve it).

It would have been easier if he hadn't found her attractive. Usually the sort of woman who makes such blatant advances is eminently resistible. But in Felicity's case, she was not impelled by the plain girl's need to take the initiative, but by youthful enthusiasm and social immaturity. Charles was determined to resist her.

But as the alcohol warmed and relaxed him, he could feel lust beginning to take the upper hand. When he had finished her excellent chocolate mousse, he made an immense effort of will, and rose to his feet. 'I think I'd better be off now. I'm doing my big scene tomorrow. Perhaps I can ring for a minicab.'

She didn't move. 'What's your big scene?'

'My death. The death of Tick, the deformed coachman shot down by Sir Rupert Cartland, as he rushed along the gallery to capture the abysmal Lady Laetitia Winthrop.'

'You needn't go.'

'I must.' Well done, Charles. The Festival of Light would be proud of you.

Felicity rose very deliberately from the table, walked towards him, and pressing her body close to his, kissed his lips. Charles stood like a carved idol receiving the homage of the faithful. He gave nothing. 'I think I had better go.'

'Why?' She used that word disconcertingly often.

'Well, I . . . um . . . you know . . .' It was difficult to think of a good reason at a moment like this.

'If you don't find me attractive, you can say so. I'll survive.'

'It's not that. You gotta believe me, it's not that.' He dropped into American to hide his confusion.

'Are you worried about my age?'

'Yes. Amongst other things.'

'Listen, Charles. I am eighteen, which is not only two years above the age of consent, but is also now the age of majority. And I'm on the Pill, so you needn't worry about that.'

Her frankness was very confusing. Charles felt himself blushing. 'Um . . . you mean, you're not a virgin?'

Her short derisive laugh made him feel suitably patronised. 'Charles, I lost my virginity when I was twelve, and since then quite a few other things have happened.' The weakness of the ending of her sentence again revealed her youth.

Charles could feel his resolve slackening, but made one last effort. 'I'm too old for you, Felicity.'

'You're not as old as the man who had me first.'

'Oh. Who was he?'

'Marius Steen.'

* * *

The next day Charles was feeling elated. He had parted from Felicity on good terms after breakfast; she had returned to continue her courses. He'd rung Jacqui, and she was fine. To crown the day, he was going to film the death of Tick, the deformed coachman, and he enjoyed a bit of ham as much as any other actor.

They rehearsed the scene in the morning. Tick crept in through the window of the dining room and surprised Lady Laetitia Winthrop playing at her virginals (a likely story). He carried a rope with which to bind her. When she saw him, she let out a little cry (that bit took ages to rehearse: every bit that required Lady Laetitia to do more than flash her tits took ages), then turned and ran to the end of the room. Tick cried out, 'Not so fast, my proud beauty!' (really), and pursued her. She ran up the stairs to the minstrels' gallery with Tick in breathy pursuit. (That was filmed in long-shot from the other end of the room). Then a quick close-up of Lady Laetitia cowering panic-stricken against the wall. (That took a long time too. 'For Christ's sake,' said Jean-Luc Roussel, 'panic-stricken, not bleeding constipated! Imagine he's going to cut yer tits off!') Then a long-shot from behind Sir Rupert Cartland's shoulder as he forced open the dining-room door, saw the scene of Tick advancing menacingly on his beloved (or 'that silly bitch,' as he always called her off the set), raised his pistol, cried, 'No, you monster' and shot the deformed coachman. Tick stopped and staggered. Cut to close-up of blood trickling from his face as he fell against the rail. Cut to shot of stuntman falling backwards over rail to the floor.

When the rehearsal was finally over, they adjourned for lunch in the billiard room, where the covers on the tables had a splendid buffet laid on them. Charles piled up his plate and sat on his own in the corner. To his surprise, two men came over and joined him. They were called Jem and Eric; he recognised them; they'd been around since the filming started. Jem was one of those burly figures who proliferate on film-sets. His role was ill-defined except to himself and other members of his union, but he spent most of his time carting scenery around and moving heavy props into position. Eric was a smaller, colourless man who worked in some clerical capacity in the production office. They never said much on the set except to each other. Nobody took much notice of them or expected them to start up any form of conversation, so Charles was surprised when Eric addressed him by name.

'Yes?'

'There's a bit of a query on your contract,' said Eric in his flat London voice. 'Been a typing error on some of them. Maybe on yours. Anyway, we want to send a duplicate just in case. It doesn't change anything.'

'OK. Fine.'

'Don't seem to have your address. Where should we send it to?'

Charles gave him the address of Maurice Skellern Artistes.

'Oh, we want it signed quickly. Wouldn't it be better if we sent it to your home?'

'No. My agent deals with all that kind of stuff.'

'Oh. Oh well, fine. We'll send it there then.' And Jem and Eric wandered off.

It gave Charles an uncomfortable feeling. True, it might be a genuine enquiry, but it could be Nigel Steen relating him to Jacqui for the first time. If so, a new hiding-place must be found quickly. Yes, it was fishy. If a new contract had to be signed urgently, why hadn't Eric brought it to him there and then, rather than posting it? Still, there was a bit of breathing space. Maurice would never give away the Hereford Road address and very few people knew it. Even friends. Charles hated the place so much he always arranged meetings in pubs, and never took anyone there. But the incident was disquieting.

He soon forgot it as the filming restarted. It was painfully slow. Lady Laetitia had forgotten all she'd been taught in the morning and everything had to be rehearsed again. Charles felt he would scream at another repetition of 'Not so fast, my proud beauty!' But progress was made and, shot by shot, Jean-Luc Roussel was satisfied. ('Not bleeding marvellous, but it'll have to do if we're going to get it all in before the bleeding electricians have their bleeding break.')

Eventually Lady Laetitia and Tick made it to the minstrels' gallery. Then there was a long break as the cameras were set up for the dramatic shot over Sir Rupert Cartland's shoulder. Make-up girls fluttered in and out with powder puffs. Electricians looked at their watches and slowly pushed their arc lights about. Jem handed Sir Rupert his props. Sir Rupert complained that one of the buckles on his shoes was loose (the shot was only going to reveal his right ear and shoulder). Eventually all was ready. '*The Zombie Walks*: Scene 143, Take One'—the clapper-board clapped shut. Tick advanced on his prey cowering constipated against the wall. The doors of the dining room burst open. Sir Rupert Cartland cried, 'No, you monster,' and a shot rang out.

Charles Paris felt a searing pain as a bullet ripped into his flesh. He crumpled up in agony.

CHAPTER FIFTEEN

POOR OLD BARON!

Charles really thought he was dying when he woke up the next morning. Cold tremors of fear kept shaking his whole body. It wasn't the wound that worried him, though his arm still ached as though a steam-hammer had landed on it. Head and body felt disconnected and the foul taste in his mouth seemed to his waking mind a symptom of some terrible decay creeping over him from within.

For once it wasn't alcohol, or at least not just alcohol. The Battle Hospital in Reading had given him a sedative to take if necessary when he was discharged. The wound was clean and dressed; there was no point in keeping him inside with such a shortage of hospital beds. So the film company organised a car to take him from Reading to Pangbourne. Jean-Luc Roussel himself had come to the hospital and fretted and fluttered about like a true Cockney sparrow. Steenway Productions was very anxious about the the injury; it is the sort of thing all film companies dread, because it inevitably leads to enormous claims for compensation.

They had tried to find out how the accident had happened. The gun was a genuine late-Victorian revolver (another anachronism in a film so full of them that its period could be any time between 1700 and 1900). How live bullets had got into it no one could imagine. The props people said they hadn't touched it; it had come like that from the place of hiring. The hiring firm were very affronted when rung up, and assured the film company that they only ever supplied blanks. No doubt a further investigation would follow.

The thought of substantial compensation didn't comfort Charles much. It was the taste of death in his mouth that preoccupied him. He staggered out of bed and cleaned his teeth, but the taste was still there. He put his hands on the marine blue wash-basin and his body sagged forward. The face in the mirror of the marine blue bathroom cabinet looked terrified and ill. Partly he knew it was last night's sedative, coupled with a large slug of Miles's Chivas Regal. Coming after the sleepless night spent with Felicity, it was bound to affect him pretty badly. But more than that it was the shock, a feeling that left his body as cold as ice, and sent these involuntary convulsions through him.

He started to dress, but almost passed out with the pain from his arm. To steady himself he sank down on the side of the bed. At that moment, Juliet came into the bedroom. 'Daddy, are you all right? I heard you moving and—'

Charles nodded weakly.

'You look ghastly,' she said.

'I feel it. Here, would you help me get dressed? This bloody arm . . . I can't do anything.'

Very gently his daughter started to help him into his clothes. As she bent to pick up his trousers, she looked just like Frances. 'Daughter and wife whom I'll leave when I die'—the phrase came into his maudlin thoughts and he started crying convulsively.

'Daddy, Daddy.'

'It's just the shock,' he managed to get out between sobs.

'Daddy, calm down.' But his body had taken control and he couldn't calm down.

'Daddy, get back to bed. I'll call the doctor.'

'NO . . . I can't go back to bed, because I've got to get to London. I've got to get . . . to London. I've got to get to London.' Suddenly the repetition seemed very funny and his sobs changed to ripples of high-pitched giggles. The situation became funnier and funnier and he lay back on the bed shaken by deep gasps of laughter.

Juliet talked calmingly to no avail. Suddenly her hand lashed out and slapped his face. Hard. It had the desired effect. The convulsions stopped and Charles lay back exhausted. He still felt ill, but the hysterics seemed to have relaxed him a bit. Juliet helped him back under the bedclothes. 'I'm going to get the doctor,' she said, and left the room.

Charles dropped immediately into a deep sleep where lumbering Thurber cartoon figures with guns in their hands chased him through a landscape of pastel green, dotted with red flowers. There was no menace in their attack. He was running hand in hand with a girl who was Juliet or Felicity, but wearing Frances's old white duffel coat. They stopped at a launderette. The girl, whose face was now Jacqui's, clasped his arm and said, 'It's a pity the *Battleship Potemkin* is booked for Easter.' She kept hold of his arm and shook it till it became elastic and extended out of its socket like a conjuror's string of handkerchiefs.

'Mr Paris.' Charles opened his eyes warily, disgruntled at being dragged out of his dream. 'Mr Paris. I am Dr Lefeuvre.'

'Hello,' said Charles sleepily.

'It's rather difficult you not being one of my regular patients, but since your daughter is, I'm stretching a point. She's told me about your accident yesterday, but I gather that's not what's troubling you?' The voice had a slight Australian twang. Charles looked at Dr Lefeuvre. A man in his mid-thirties with dull auburn hair and a freckled face behind rectangular metal-rimmed glasses. He had very long hands, which were also covered in freckles and sported three gold rings.

'I don't know, Doctor. I just feel very weak and ill.'

'The arm's all right?'

'It feels bruised, but that's all.'

'Only to be expected. Let's just have a look at the dressing.' He cast his eye expertly over the bandage on Charles's arm. 'It's been very well done. When are you due to go back to the hospital?'

'They'll change the dressing next Monday.'

'That seems fine. I won't meddle with it then. But otherwise you're feeling run down and ill. It's probably just shock.'

'Yes.'

'I'd better have a look at you.' And the doctor began the time-honoured ritual of taking temperature and pulses. In fact, Charles felt better now. His body had regained some warmth and the sleep had relaxed him. He just felt as if he'd run full tilt into a brick wall.

Dr Lefeuvre looked at the temperature. 'Hmm. That's strange.'

'What?'

'You seem to have a slight temperature. Just over a hundred. That's not really consistent with shock. Let's take your shirt off. There. Not hurting the arm?'

'No.'

'Hmm.' The doctor started probing and tapping. 'Let's have a look at your throat. Open. There. Tongue down. No, down. Yes. Is your throat at all sore?'

'A bit. Sort of foul taste in my mouth.'

'Yes. Hm. That's strange. You haven't been in contact with German measles recently?'

'Not to my knowledge, no.'

'No. Hmmm. Because, on a cursory examination, I would say that is what you've got. There's a slight rash on your chest, hardly visible. The temperature and the sore throat are consistent.'

'Oh. Well, what should I do about it?'

'Nothing much. It's not very serious. If you're feeling

bad, stay in bed. It'll clear up in a couple of days. You don't have to rush back to work, do you?'

'No, they've reorganised the shooting schedule.'

'Oh.' Dr Lefeuvre obviously didn't understand what that meant, but equally obviously it didn't interest him much either. 'Look, I'll prescribe some penicillin.' He scribbled on his pad. 'You'd better check with Battle Hospital, tell them you're going to take it. Just in case they want to put you on something else.'

'Fine.'

'Good. Oh. I'd better just have your address and National Health Number for the records.' Charles gave them, digging the number out of a 1972 diary which was so full of useful information he'd never managed to get rid of it.

'Right.' Dr Lefeuvre gathered his things together and prepared to leave.

'So there's nothing special I should do? Just rest?'

'Yes. You'll feel better in a couple of days. The rest won't do the arm any harm either.'

'OK.'

'Oh, there is one thing of course with German measles.'

'Yes.'

'You mustn't be in contact with anyone who's expecting a baby. If a woman gets German measles while she's pregnant, it can have very bad effects on the unborn child.'

Charles dressed with Juliet's help (he didn't like staying in bed alone) and rang Jacqui as soon as the doctor had left. He didn't mention the 'accident' at Bloomwater because it would only upset her. In fact, she sounded particularly cheerful; it was the first morning she had woken up with no trace of sickness, and was cheered at the thought of entering the 'blooming' phase of pregnancy. No, nothing disturbing had happened. Nobody had rung. She was quite happy in her little prison.

Charles felt fairly confident of her safety for the time being. Though the shooting on the film set, if it wasn't accidental, implied that Nigel Steen knew of his involvement, he still might not have realised the direct connection with Jacqui, and certainly was no nearer getting the Hereford Road address. But she would have to be moved soon. Charles determined to ring Frances and ask her to take the girl in. It would be a strange coupling, but Frances wouldn't refuse. He explained to Jacqui about the German measles.

'Oh no, for God's sake keep away from me,' she said. 'The child is born blind or something terrible.'

'Don't worry. I'll stay away.'

'How long are you infectious?'

'I should be better in two or three days. But I don't know how long the quarantine period is. It's probably just as well I haven't been near you for the last week. Don't worry though. I won't come back till I'm quite clear of it. I'll ring Dr Lefeuvre and check.'

'Who?'

'Dr Lefeuvre.'

'Australian?'

'Yes.'

'Good God.'

'Why. Do you know him?'

'Yes. He was the one who did my abortion in the summer.'

'What? But it wasn't a legal one, was it?'

'No. Marius got Nigel to fix it up?'

'Was Lefeuvre the family doctor?'

'I suppose so. Marius didn't talk about doctors. He kept saying he was never ill.'

'So it was probably Lefeuvre who was called in when Marius died.'

'Yes, it was. He was at the inquest.'

'He was? Jacqui, for Christ's sake. Why didn't you tell me this before?'

'I didn't think it was important. Is it?'

'Jesus!' But there was no time to explain. And no point in worrying her. 'Jacqui, just sit tight. Don't worry about anything.' He slammed the phone down. 'Juliet, can I have your car keys? I've got to go up to London immediately.'

Juliet emerged dazed from the kitchen area. 'But you can't take the Cortina. Miles'll be furious.'

'I haven't got time to worry about Miles. Give me the keys.'

Juliet was amazed by the sudden force of his personality and held out the keys, as if hypnotised. 'But, Daddy, you can't drive with that arm.'

'I bloody can.'

CHAPTER SIXTEEN

BACK AT THE FIRESIDE

Being back in London was a disappointment. The mad drive up the M4 with pain like barbed hooks turning in his arm had all been for nothing. He had screeched to a halt in the residents' parking bay in an unimpressed Hereford Road, let himself in, banged on his own door and, keeping his distance, ordered Jacqui to go off to the pictures for the afternoon. Then he'd driven round to the surgery of Drs Singh and Gupta, with whom he was registered, only to find that both were out on their rounds. He rushed to St Mary's Hospital, Paddington, and, after the hours of waiting that are statutory in hospitals, finally persuaded a callow houseman to examine him and pronounce him clear of German measles. It was evident from the young man's circumspect excitement that he thought he'd got his first genuine schizophrenic hypochondriac. Charles ended up with a clean bill of health and a parking ticket.

As he sat in his drab room in Hereford Road, it all seemed a bit futile. The dark fears of the morning had subsided into childish fantasies. He felt he should be watching the road from behind the curtains, waiting for the badmen to arrive at High Noon, while in the background a voice intoned 'Do not forsake me, O my darling.' But since his windows faced the back of the house, it was impossible. And in the familiar banality of his room thoughts of approaching badmen seemed ridiculous. He just felt tired and ill again. The excitements of the day had put him back considerably. Pain throbbed in his arm with agonising regularity. He felt himself drifting asleep.

Suddenly the phone rang. Swedish feet in wooden sandals clumped down the stairs past his door, then up again, paused, knocked, said 'Telephone' and continued back to their room.

He went down and picked up the dangling receiver. 'Hello.'

'Hello. It's Joanne Menzies.'

'Oh. Hi.'

'Charles, can we meet and talk? About Marius's death.'

'Yes, sure. Have you got anything new?'

'Not really. But I'm just convinced there was something fishy going on.'

'Yes. There are a lot of things that don't fit. When do you want to meet? After work?'

'I'm not at work.'

'Oh.'

'I came back after Christmas to the news that my services were no longer required by Mr Nigel Steen. A year's salary in lieu of notice.'

'That's a substantial pay-off.'

'Yes. Hush-money, no doubt. Where shall we meet?'

'Do you mind coming round here? I'm not very well.'

'Fine. What's the address?' Charles gave it. 'I'll be round straight away.' He put the phone down and had a moment's doubt. Was he wise to give Joanne Menzies his address? She seemed straight enough, but her motives weren't absolutely clear. Oh well, if she told Nigel Steen, fair enough. Charles's suspicions of Dr Lefeuvre made him think his address was already common knowledge. At least he was here now, and could supervise moving Jacqui to another hideaway. He rang Frances's number to make his strange request, but there was no reply. It was only five o'clock. No doubt she was supervising the school debating society or another of her public-spirited activities.

Joanne Menzies arrived quickly and they started talking over a glass of whisky. Charles gave the shortest possible explanation of his sling—'an accident on the film set.' He didn't want to voice any suspicions until he felt a bit surer of Joanne's allegiances. 'So. What do you think is fishy?'

'No one big thing, Charles. Just a lot of dubious details.'

'Like . . . ?'

'Like the way Nigel lied over that Saturday night, all the subterfuge over the petrol in the Datsun. Like the way he's been behaving since his father's death—and the week before, come to that—'

'How's he been behaving?'

'Very twitchy. Jumps whenever the phone rings. As if there's something he's frightened of.'

'What else?'

'The way I've been dismissed. All right, I was Marius's personal assistant and there's no reason to assume that Nigel would want to take me over in the same role. But it was rather sudden. And a year's salary is excessive—out of character too for someone as mean as Nigel.'

'Hmm. So you think that Nigel murdered Marius?'

'That's the obvious thing to think.'

'Except for the findings of the inquest.'

'Yes.' Joanne spoke with the same contempt Jacqui had shown for the high achievements of forensic science.

'And the fact that Nigel had no motive. It was in his interests that his father should live at least until the seven years were up.' Joanne's face revealed that she didn't know about the gift, so Charles gave a brief résumé of the legal position. He finished up, 'You know, we are not the only people who are suspicious of Nigel and would attribute any crime to him. But the fact remains that, in the matter of Marius Steen's death, we have not a solitary shred of evidence to go on. Just prejudice and dislike.'

'Yes. I'm sure he's done something, though.' Her conviction was reminiscent of Jacqui's, overriding little details like facts.

'All right, Joanne, let's talk through it all again. Actually, one thing you said interested me. You said Nigel was twitchy the week before the murder—I mean, the death.'

'Yes.'

'I thought he was in Streatley that week.'

'Only part of it. He went down on the Thursday to go through some business things with Marius, then came back on the Friday late afternoon—just after you came round about your play. Was that another blind, by the way?'

''Fraid so.'

'Why?'

'Too complicated to explain.' He didn't want to bring in the Sweets and the implied charge of murder against the dead man. 'So look, let's trace through the movements of the two of them. Where were they on the Sunday, that'd be what . . . ?'

'The 2nd of December.'

'Right.'

'I think they were both in Orme Gardens. Then Marius drove to Streatley that night to read the scripts on his own.'

'Was that unexpected?'

'No, he'd been talking about it. He'd noticed a slight waning in the receipts on *Sex of One* . . . though I think it was just the power crisis and the railways. Anyway, he felt he had to make a decision on the next show for the King's.'

'And when he did one of these script-reading sessions, he used to cut himself off completely?'

'Yes. Just switch on the Ansaphone.'

'I see. So when did you last speak to him?'

'Small hours of Sunday morning. At the *Sex of One* . . . party.'

'Oh yes. A thousand performances. Ugh. Let's continue their movements. Marius is in Streatley. Where's Nigel, say on the Monday morning? Milton Buildings?'

'No, he came in after lunch.'

'Was that unusual?'

'No. Particularly considering the late night we'd all had on the Saturday.'

'Right. Incidentally, how was Marius at the party?'

'In marvellous form—leaping around like a boy of twenty. Dancing with all the girls.' The pride was evident in her voice.

'Including you.'

'Yes.'

'You loved him, didn't you?'

'Yes.'

'Did you know he was contemplating remarriage?'

'I knew.'

'Did you mind?'

'Yes, but if it made him happy . . . If Marius wanted something there was no point in trying to stop his getting it.'

'No.' Her answers sounded perfectly honest. 'Let's continue our tracing movements. Which car did Nigel go down in on the Thursday?'

'His own. The Interceptor. It was after that that he complained about the brakes to Morrison.'

'Right. And then he goes down again in secret on the Saturday in the Datsun. The Datsun, the Datsun. You know there's something at the back of my mind about that Datsun and I can't think what it is.' He looked round the room for inspiration. It was an untidy mess. Jacqui's occupation hadn't improved it; she wasn't the sort of girl who immediately revolutionised a place and gave it a woman's touch; she just spread her belongings over the widest possible area. A flouncy negligée and a pair of tights lay over one chair; the tiny television was perched on another; a soggy packet of frozen spinach lay beside the gas-ring; on the crumpled candlewick of the bed an *Evening Standard* was open at the entertainments' page so she could decide which film to go and see.

A thought suddenly illuminated Charles's brain like a flash of lightning. 'That's it. The *Evening Standard*.'

'What?' Joanne was left floundering as his mind raced on. Very clearly he saw himself standing in the BBC Club with Sherlock Forster and hearing the name of Marius Steen, the name that had come to dominate his life. When was that? It was a Monday. Yes, Monday the 3rd of December. After that terrible play. And what had the paper said? Something about Marius not using the Rolls, but sticking to the Datsun. Oh, if only he could remember the details.

There was one person who could help. Johnny Smart, who'd been at Oxford with him and edited one of the university magazines, landed what seemed then an amazing job on the *Evening Standard*. In the years since he'd sunk into alcoholic indifference in the same job, which at his present age was less amazing. With a murmured excuse to Joanne, Charles rushed to the telephone and rang the paper. Fortunately Johnny was still there—a stroke of luck considering that the pubs were open. In rather breathless fashion, Charles explained that he wanted to find out who researched and wrote an article about the petrol crisis in a late edition on Monday 3rd of December.

Johnny thought he could probably find out. It was bound to be one of the young reporters. Why didn't Charles come down and join them at Mother Bunch's? A lot would be down there at this time of night. He'd be there himself except that the newsroom was on sodding tenterhooks waiting to see if Heath would call a sodding snap election and they'd have to bring out a sodding slip edition. He'd be down in half an hour though.

Just as Charles put the phone down, Jacqui returned. She had been to see *Enter the Dragon* and started to tell him all about the code of *kung fu* as he hurried her upstairs. Joanne recognised Jacqui the moment the dark glasses came off and Charles felt the room temperature drop as the two women faced each other. Still, he hadn't time to worry about that. Leaving strict instructions to Joanne to stay there at all costs and to both of them under no account to let anyone in, he hurried to the Cortina and set off for Fleet Street.

Reporters are proverbially heavy drinkers, and it took a few bottles of *bonhomie* with Johnny Smart before Charles could actually get down to the business for which he had come. He sat in the broad circle of young journalists in Mother Bunch's Wine House and, with the rest of them, sank glass after glass of red wine. Eventually Johnny drew him to one side with a shock-haired young reporter who sported horn-rimmed glasses and a velvet bow tie. His name was Keith Battrick-Jones. Charles explained his mission.

'Bloody hell,' said Keith Battrick-Jones. 'Done a lot of stories since then. I don't know if I can remember that far back. When was it?'

'Monday 3rd December. Six, seven weeks ago. It was a sort of round-up of people's reactions to the petrol crisis. Pictures and comments. There was Steen . . .' The boy looked blank. '. . . and some footballer . . .' Still blank. '. . . and a leggy girl on a bike—'

'Oh shit. I remember. Yes. Crappy idea, wasn't it? Somebody thought of it at an editorial conference, and Muggins here had to ring round all these celebrities to get comments. As usual, the interesting people told me to piss off, and I ended up with the same old circle of publicity seekers.'

'Can you remember phoning Marius Steen?'

'No, I don't think I can. If it was Monday morning, I must have had a skinful the night before. No, I . . . oh, just a minute though. I remember. I rang through and I got some old berk being facetious on an Ansaphone. So I told the machine what it was about, and moved on to a golfer and one of the Black and White minstrels.'

'But Steen did phone back?'

'Yes. Made some fatuous comment about using the smaller car. Well, we'd got a library picture of him, so we put it in.'

'And you are sure it was Marius Steen himself who spoke to you?'

'I don't know. I've never met the bloke.'

'Was it the same voice as the one on the Ansaphone?'

'Oh no. It was much more cultured. And younger.'

CHAPTER SEVENTEEN

THE BROKER'S MEN

Charles had a lot of wine inside him as he drove along the Strand on his way back, but he was thinking with extraordinary clarity. Suddenly Nigel had two secret trips to Streatley to explain, not one. If he had been at the *Sex of One . . .* party, he must have driven down some time between the small hours of the Sunday morning and when he rang Keith Battrick-Jones on the Monday morning. That was, of course, assuming that he had gone down on his own. It was possible that he had been in the Rolls with his father on the Sunday night.

If that were the case, and Charles's other conjecture was correct, he must have witnessed Marius shooting Bill Sweet on the roadside at Theale. That might well explain the twitchiness which Joanne had noticed during the ensuing week. Possibly Nigel had shot Bill Sweet himself? But no, that was nonsense. He had nothing to do with the Sally Nash affair, and the Sweets represented no threat to him. If anyone had committed murder on the lonely turn-off from the M4, it must have been Marius.

At Hyde Park Corner, a taxi travelling from Knightsbridge suddenly cut across the front of the Cortina and Charles had to slam on all his brakes. The shock jarred every bone in his body and he felt as if he was about to pass out. There was nothing else coming. He swung the car across the yellow line and stopped by the marble colonnade at the roadside. His body was in agony. Slowly the total blinding pain broke down into individual centres of hurt. First there was his arm, with its bone bruised by the bullet. That pain seemed to swell and swamp the others. Then there were the bruises on his knees and elbows that he'd received from the fall over the trip-wire at Jacqui's. And then, lower down the league of pain, there was the dull ache of an old bruise on his ankle.

Suddenly, he saw in his mind the utility room at Streatley and a scattered pile of boxes. Some words of Gerald Venables' reverberated in his head. Dr Lefeuvre's role came clearly defined into focus, and Charles Paris knew what Nigel Steen's crime was.

As he walked up the stairs at Hereford Road, he was glowing with the intellectual perfection of it. Not the intellectual perfection of the crime—that was a shabby affair—but the intellectual perfection of his conclusion. Suddenly, given one fact, all the others clicked neatly into position. As he drove back, he had tried each element individually, and none of them broke the pattern. He was looking forward to spelling it all out to Jacqui and Joanne. Actual evidence was still a bit short on the ground (burning the vicious letter to Jacqui and the Sweet photographs had shown a regrettable lack of detective instinct). But he felt sure facts would come, now the basic riddle was solved.

The door of his room was open, the lock plate hanging loose. A cold feeling trickled into his stomach as he went inside. It was dark. He switched on the light. A body lay tied, gagged and struggling on the floor by the bed. Joanne. There was no sign of Jacqui.

He fumbled with the knots of Jacqui's tights which had been tied cruelly round Joanne's mouth. She gave a little gasp of pain as he tightened to release them, and then she was free to talk. 'Two men . . . someone must have let them in the front door . . . they took Jacqui . . .'

'Did you see them?'

'They had stockings over their heads. One was big and burly, the other was smaller . . .'

'Yes. I know who they are.' He cut her other bonds free with a kitchen knife. 'Come on. We must follow them.'

'Where to? How do we know where they've gone?'

'I think it's Streatley. And I pray to God I'm right. For the sake of Jacqui's baby.'

CHAPTER EIGHTEEN

KING RAT

They roared down the M4, fifty miles an hour limits contemptuously ignored. They swung off the motorway at Theale, past the scene of Bill Sweet's death, and on, through the dark roads, past Tidmarsh, Pangbourne, Lower Basildon, towards Strcatlcy. About a mile outside the town, the Cortina suddenly lost power and pop-popped to a stop at the roadside. 'Sod it. Bloody petrol. The whole case hinges on it, and I forget to fill up.'

'He might have a spare can,' said Joanne. But there was nothing in the boot. Miles's odious efficiency was absent when actually needed. 'I'll have to walk the rest.' Charles started off into the gloom.

'What shall I do?' Joanne's voice floated after him.

'Get the police.' He stumbled on, occasionally trying a little jogging run. His body ached all over and the wounded arm felt as if it were dropping off. The strain of the last few days was beginning to tell, and he knew he hadn't got much energy left. If it came to violence, he wasn't going to do too well. He didn't relish facing Jem and Eric (he felt sure it was they who'd carried Jacqui off).

Sweat trickled down his sides in spite of the cold. His clothes were heavy and awkward. Still the road seemed to stretch onwards endlessly, darkness replacing darkness, as he staggered forward. Occasionally a car would pass, fix him like a moth in its headlights, and then vanish.

Eventually he was at the top of the slope that led down to the little towns of Streatley and Goring, separated, like their respective counties of Berkshire and Oxfordshire, by the River Thames. Revived by the proximity of his goal, Charles hurried painfully onwards along the road to the familiar white gates. It occurred to him that being on foot was probably an advantage; a car drawing up on the gravel would be heard from the house. And in his position he needed advantages.

He opened one gate slowly, trying not to let it scrape on the gravel. Then he moved round on to the flower-bed at the side of the path, to muffle his footsteps. The house looked quiet and the same, except for a strange car parked by the front door. Again, as on the previous occasion, there was a chink of light from Marius Steen's bedroom. Was it possible that Charles's previous luck could be repeated and he'd find the door to the utility room open? Keeping to the lawn, he crept silently to the back of the garage, moved in close to the door and felt for the handle.

He closed his eyes, uttered a silent prayer and turned the knob. For a moment the door seemed firm, but then, blissfully, it gave.

He sidled into the utility room, treading with remembered caution, and reached for the light switch. The room had been tidied since his last visit. All the tins and boxes were neatly on their shelves, and, thank God, the torch was still in its place. He took it and started to put into action a plan that had half-formed in his mind during the run from the stranded Cortina.

He locked the door by which he had entered and put the key in his pocket. Then he turned his attention to the door that opened into the garage. There was no lock on that one. For a moment he stood, defeated, but then, memory working overtime, he moved into the garage, opened the door of the Rolls, and shone his torch over the dashboard. With a small grim smile of satisfaction, he went back to the utility room and looked at the power switches. He closed his eyes and memorised their positions. Then one by one, with a series of quick movements, he switched them all off. He scurried into the safety of the great car.

There was a murmur of voices from the room above, then the slow sound of people feeling their way downstairs and towards the garage. The faint glow of a match shone through the door from the house. Charles shrank into the deep upholstery of the Rolls's front seat.

There were two voices, a deep slow one, and a higher London whine. Jem and Eric, as he'd thought. They went into the utility room. Charles heard the scrape of a match, then a muttered curse. With another prayer, he turned the key in the ignition of the Rolls. It started immediately. He found first gear and eased the great machine slowly forward until it hit the utility room door, closed it, and pinned it fast. Then he pulled on the hand-brake and leapt out.

The hammering of Jem and Eric followed him, as he rushed upstairs with the torch to Marius Steen's bedroom. As he entered it, one of the prisoners found the switches, and the lights came on again.

The scene which they revealed was an ugly one. On the bed, Jacqui lay unconscious. She was on a sheet, naked with her legs spread apart. Another sheet was crumpled over her thighs. On either side of her, blinking in the sudden light, were Nigel Steen and Dr Lefeuvre. Laid out on a cloth on a stool were a row of bright instruments. A scalpel gleamed in the doctor's long freckled hand.

Nigel was the first to speak. 'Charles Paris . . . You are taking a very great risk.'

'Nothing to some of the risks you've taken, Steen.'

There was a silence. Nobody moved. Then came the sound of renewed battering from downstairs. Dr Lefeuvre dropped his scalpel with the other instruments, gathered them up in the cloth and put them in his bag. 'I'm leaving, Steen.'

Panic flashed into Nigel's face. 'You can't do that. I need your help.'

'No, Steen. Get out of this one on your own.'

'You've got to help me.'

'No.'

'You did the other things for me.'

'Not for you. For money.'

'I'll tell the police what you've done.'

'I think that unlikely. It might involve too much explanation of your own activities. Anyway, I will have left the country by then. I'd planned to go back to Australia when I'd made enough. And, thanks to you'—he tapped the case—'that time's come.'

'But—'

'Goodbye, Steen.' Dr Lefeuvre left the room. Neither Charles nor Nigel spoke as they heard his footsteps on the stairs, the slam of the front door, the gates being opened, and his car departing in a scurry of gravel.

'What do you want, Paris? Money?' said Nigel Steen suddenly.

'No.'

'I could give you a lot. I'll pay for silence.'

'And then set your thugs on me the first time my back's turned. No, thank you.'

'Then what do you want?'

'Just to talk. See if what I think is correct—until the police come.'

'I see. Come through here.'

Nigel Steen led Charles, with what was meant to be a lordly gesture, into the study next door. He sat behind the desk and offered the older man a plush leather seat. 'Well now,' in deliberately even tones, 'what is all this about the police? Shouldn't I be calling them to get you, as a common house-breaker?'

'You could try, but I think they'd find your case more interesting.'

'Do you? Why? What are you accusing me of? The inquest has already proved I didn't murder my father.'

'I know. That's not what I am accusing you of.'

Nigel's face went pale. 'What are you accusing me of then?'

'I'll tell you. Stop me if I'm wrong. This is the story as I see it. On Saturday 1st December, your father Marius Steen went to the party on stage at the King's Theatre to celebrate the one thousandth performance of *Sex of One and Half a Dozen of the Other*. He enjoyed the party, danced, drank and generally had a whale of a time.

'The following day, Sunday 2nd December, your father, because of his exertions, suffered a second heart attack, and died. You, with a shrewd sense of your own advantage, realised that you were now liable to pay one hell of a lot of estate duty on your father's gift to you because of his inconvenient death; but that if he had died a fortnight later it would be six and not five years since the property was made over to you. If you could maintain the illusion that your father was still alive for another fortnight you would be saving—say the property was worth one million—about £240,000. A quarter of a million pounds has been the motive for far worse crimes than the one you contemplated.

'Obviously, you needed help. And it was to hand. Dear Dr Lefeuvre, who had already arranged at least one abortion for you, was always susceptible to bribery, or, if not that, to blackmail. All he had to do was to come round when you called and sign the death certificate with all particulars correct. Except the date.

'Now there was a problem, of course. The police might want to see the body; the undertaker certainly would. How to preserve it? Why not the good old deep-freeze? Keep the old man in there, get him out in good time to defrost, maybe even put him in a hot bath to remove any traces of his preservation. And there you are.

'So, late on the Sunday night, with your father's body propped up in the Rolls, you drive to Streatley, move a few boxes out of the deep-freeze and put your father in. On the Monday, after making one mistake by phoning the *Evening Standard*—and I can sympathise with your reasons for that mistake; after all, it was a heaven-sent opportunity to assert your father's continued existence—anyway, after that you get a train back to London . . . I'm guessing there, but it's not important.

'So it was all set up, and your father's known habit of shutting himself up with his scripts made the deception all the easier. The only fly in the ointment was Jacqui. If she kept on trying to contact your father, it could be awkward. Still, she was on her own, and not very brave. A little intimidation should keep her quiet. An anonymous letter, and, when that didn't work, Jem and Eric doing her flat over. Easy.

'On the Thursday you return to Streatley, to maintain the myth of your father's continuing business interests; and perhaps to check a few details with Dr Lefeuvre. Or even to put the pressure on him, maybe?

'Then on the Saturday, something rattles you. You lose your nerve, drive down to Streatley in secret, change the tape in your father's Ansaphone, prepare the body and move your whole schedule forward a week. That, I must confess, is the bit I don't understand. By doing that you made the whole crime worthless. You were losing money. No doubt you had your reasons.

'But when the new will came to light, you were liable to lose even more money. So, seeing the flaw in its hastily drawn up provisions, you started your vendetta against Jacqui's child, a vendetta that Dr Lefeuvre was about to complete when I arrived. No doubt, before that you used the cruder talents of Jem and Eric. Certainly, when you realised my connection with the case at Bloomwater, they were the bully-boys you turned on to me.

'Well, I think that sums up most of my conclusions. How am I doing?'

He looked up at Nigel Steen. The man's face was white and mean and he was pointing an automatic pistol at Charles's chest. But he still tried to maintain some shreds of panache. 'Very good,' he said slowly. 'How did you know about the boxes in the freezer?'

'Ah, I must confess I have been in this house before. Just before your dramatic discovery of your father's corpse, I . . . er . . . fell over the boxes. They were heavy and had the words "Do not refreeze" written on them, but I didn't immediately realise the significance of that. Sorry. I was a bit slow on the uptake.'

'I see. Well, since I am going to kill you anyway—an intruder in my house, I met you, drew my gun; you attacked me and in the ensuing fight the gun went off, unfortunately killing you—I—'

'If that's as successful as your other crimes, I think I'm fairly safe.'

'Quiet!' Nigel waved the gun. 'Let me fill in the details. One thing you were wrong about is the extent of my crime. The things you describe could be classed as fraud and harassment maybe, but in fact there is a murder involved.'

'Yes, I know.' Steen looked at him open-mouthed, robbed of the drama of his pronouncement, as Charles continued, 'Bill Sweet's murder.'

'Whose?'

'Bill Sweet, the man who was found shot dead at Theale.'

'Oh, was that his name? I didn't know.'

'You mean you didn't know his connection with your father?'

'No. Was there one?'

'What happened, Steen?'

'We came off the M4 and suddenly there was this maniac in the middle of the road, flagging us down. I swerved to avoid him and hit his silly little car. I tried to drive on, but he came at me with some story of having run out of petrol. Then he looked in the car, saw my father crumpled up and started to speak. I panicked and shot him. I went through his pockets—for some reason they were full of dirty pictures. I took them and his wallet and threw the lot, with the gun, into the river.'

'Why his wallet?'

'To disguise his identity. I don't know. I panicked. I wanted to forget all about him—pretend it hadn't happened.'

'And that's why you haven't moved the Rolls since that night. You even left your father's keys in it. You seem to do rather a lot of panicking, don't you? Not a very impressive criminal.'

'If my plan had worked, it would have been a masterstroke. To save a quarter of a million—that's the sort of thing my father used to do.' The envy in his voice was almost pathetic.

'But you could never do what your father did, could you, Nigel? Business, women, even crime. You just never made it.' Nigel Steen's knuckles whitened around the gun and Charles uttered another silent prayer. He seemed to be getting very religious all of a sudden. 'Because you never had the guts to carry anything through,' he continued. 'Why didn't you carry this one through?'

'Because of you, you little sod.' Nigel spat the words out.

'Me?'

'Yes, you and your bloody Detective-Sergeant McWhirter business. When you rang up that Saturday and checked the registration of the Rolls, I thought the police were on to the Theale murder.'

'Good Lord.' Charles had completely forgotten about the first entrance of McWhirter. It came back to him vaguely. And that had actually ruined Nigel's crime. Charles could have chosen any excuse for the phone call and it was pure chance that he had lighted on the meaningless 'number-plate racket!' 'So that's what made you drive down in the Datsun, and move the plan forward, and lose a quarter of a million pounds?'

'Yes.'

'Good Lord.' Charles was absolutely flabbergasted, but he hadn't really got time to analyse his reactions. Nigel was still pointing a rather businesslike gun at him. 'Nigel, I'd put that thing away. The police are coming. You stand a chance as things stand at the minute. They need never find out about Sweet's murder. Just get you on the other charges.'

'I don't believe you, Paris. You're bluffing. There aren't any police coming.'

'There are.' Charles prayed that he was speaking the truth. 'Joanne Menzies is getting them.'

'So, she was involved with you. The bitch.'

'I think you'd better hand that gun over, Nigel.' Charles rose to his feet.

'Don't move! I'll shoot you!' Nigel held the gun away from him, as if he was afraid of the bang it would make. Charles felt himself sweating.

He tried desperately to control his voice. 'No, Nigel, you won't shoot me. This is cold blood, Nigel. Something you've got to think about. Not like shooting Sweet in a moment of blind panic. Not like doing it by remote control, having Jem set up a trip-wire. This is you committing a crime, Nigel.'

The two men faced each other. Their eyes were interlocked and the gun pointed directly at Charles's heart. The pause seemed endless.

Suddenly the doorbell rang. Nigel tensed as if to fire, and Charles closed his eyes. Then he heard the clatter of the gun falling on to the desk. He looked at Nigel Steen and saw the glint of tears in his eyes as the young man rushed out of the door.

Charles collapsed like a glove puppet with the hand withdrawn, and stood for a long moment, sagging. The doorbell was still ringing. But before he went downstairs, he crept into Marius Steen's bedroom.

Jacqui was still unconscious, breathing heavily under the anaesthetic. Gingerly, Charles raised the sheet that lay over her thighs. There was no blood, no sign that she had been touched. As he looked down at the body he used to love, he thanked God for letting him arrive in time.

When he opened the door downstairs, he heard the roar of a motorboat leaving from the boathouse at the back. On the doorstep in front of him stood Joanne Menzies, alone. She was breathless. 'I couldn't get the police. Didn't see a phone. I've just walked from the car.'

So it had been a bluff. Charles started laughing, clear ripples of relief shaking his body. He clasped Joanne in his arms, not for love or lust, just sheer joy at being alive.

The speedboat was found splintered against Goring Bridge. It had missed the lock and been driven full-tilt down the hard steps of the weir. Nigel Steen's body was found in some weeds nearly a mile downstream. Whether the death was suicide, or a result of his natural aptitude for failure, was never established.

CHAPTER NINETEEN

FINALE AND CURTAIN CALL

Bartlemas and O'Rourke's tall Victorian house in Ideal Road, Islington, was like a chaotic museum. Every available wall surface was covered with memories of Kean and Macready; even in the lavatory the twin deities looked down beneficently on lesser mortals.

A battered life-size carving of Kean as Shylock greeted Charles as he entered the front door. The beak of a nose seemed strangely reminiscent of Marius Steen. O'Rourke took his coat. 'You know, people keep saying we ought to hang coats on Shylock's arm . . .'

'But we're sure Edmund wouldn't like it,' said Bartlemas, appearing from nowhere in a shiny apron with an advertisement for 'Camp Coffee' on it.

'No, he wouldn't. The party was really Bartlemas's idea . . .'

'Oh, I wouldn't say that, O'Rourke. Let's say we arrived at the idea mutually . . .'

'Yes, let's. Nearly everyone's here. Do go through. Bartlemas, do you want a little succour with your vinaigrette?'

'Wouldn't say no, O'Rourke. Excuse us. Titivating the goodies. Do go through . . .'

'Just toddle through . . .' They vanished in a shimmer of saxe-blue silk shirts.

The sitting-room had two walls devoted to prints of Edmund in all his greatest roles, and the other two to William. Between them, sitting with drinks, were Joanne Menzies and Gerald Venables. Gerald rose to greet Charles in typical style. 'Hello, old boy. What's the budget going to do to your savings then?'

'I haven't got any.'

'Wise feller.' Charles greeted Joanne and helped himself to a large Scotch. Gerald continued. 'Do you realise, Charles, that if these Labour Johnnies go and slap on this gift tax they're talking about, crimes like young Nigel Steen's won't be worth committing.'

'His wasn't worth committing anyway, as it turned out.'

'No. Fascinating, though, from the legal point of view. Do let me in on any more of your detective work, won't you, Charles?'

'There won't be any more, Sherlock Holmes.'

'Oh, I'm sure there will. How's the arm?'

'Healed up long ago. A nice scar though.'

'And a good story to go with it.'

The conversation drifted. Joanne talked about her new job in a concert agency. Bartlemas and O'Rourke came in and talked about the first night of Gielgud's Prospero ('Doing it again, dear') at the National. Charles felt detached and rather sad. A little parcel had arrived through the post that morning from the old people's home at Tower Hamlets. Harry Chiltern had died, and asked that all his possessions be sent to Charles. It was depressing to think that he was the closest friend that the old man had, and it stirred all the usual guilt feelings—should have gone to see him more often, and so on. The package contained a watch, a silver cigarette case, a Ronson lighter and *Stanley Matthews's Book of Football*.

It suited Charles's melancholy mood well. Nothing much seemed to be happening. He had finished shooting the rescheduled scenes of *The Zombie Walks* without meeting Felicity again. (However, the episode was not without profit, since the film company had paid very substantial compensation for his 'accident.') He was now involved in a dreary radio serial, which was driving him slowly mad with boredom. Life went on, at its usual alcoholic level.

A ring at the doorbell announced the late arrival of Jacqui, blonde again and resplendently pregnant in a long red and white flowered dress. It was so far from her usual style that Charles thought she must have undergone some violent change of personality. She greeted him slightly gushingly, and that again struck a false note.

The reason for the change soon became apparent. Given Jacqui's simple character, it could only be a man. Her escort followed her into the sitting-room. It was Bernard Walton.

'Hello, Charles. Dear boy. Joanne, darling. Hello, all you lovely people. Haven't met you, have I, sir, but I'm sure we'll get on. Tell you what, Jacqui and I were thinking of tootling on to the midnight matinée at the Parthenon after this lot. It's a charity thing—something to do with April Fools' Day. Perhaps that means it's raising money for a looney bin. Whole thing will probably be a ghastly no-no, but everyone will be there. What do you all say to the idea?'

Bartlemas and O'Rourke were terribly enthusiastic, and the others mumbled politely. Charles didn't even mumble. He knew what wasn't his scene.

The dinner was very good, though the conversation tended to be dominated by Bernard's stories of his new television series and the director who was disastrous, but disastrous. At one point, however, they did get around to Marius Steen and the circumstances of his death.

'What I never could understand,' said Gerald, 'was why Steen, who was so good with money, made such a cock-up of that final will. I mean, just leaving it to the baby, or making it dependent on the baby's survival. It's insane.'

'But you see, dear,' said Bartlemas, 'he only got that one together in a hurry . . .'

'Yes,' said O'Rourke, 'he was going to sort it all out properly when he got back to England. I mean, the so-called solicitor he found out at Saint Maxime was a boy, hardly even qualified. Just got his articles—I always think that sounds rude.' A snigger. 'So the will was only a stop-gap. But when Marius felt better, he forgot about it . . .'

'Yes. He was intending to get married, you see.'

Gerald nodded. 'Of course. Remarriage would revoke all previous wills.'

But Charles was intrigued by something O'Rourke had said. 'When Marius felt better? What did you mean by that?'

'Oh no! Didn't we tell you?' O'Rourke's eyes opened wide.

'I don't think we did, O'Rourke . . .'

'Oh well, you see, Marius had this heart attack while we were out there. Not a bad one, but it frightened him. That's why he was in such a rush about the will . . .'

'That's right. And that's why he made us witnesses and executors . . .'

'Doesn't that sound grand . . .'

'Yes, because we were the only people there . . .'

'And then he gave us the will and the other papers and he said to us, just before we toddled off to Morocco—'

'Just a minute, O'Rourke,' Charles interposed. 'What other papers?'

O'Rourke looked at Bartlemas and both of them opened their eyes wide and put their hands over their mouths in mock horror. 'Oh no, Bartlemas, we haven't . . . !'

'We have, O'Rourke . . .'

'Forgotten all about them . . .'

'Oh no!'

'Where did we have them last?'

'Well, we certainly had them when you were cleaning

that playbill of William as Lear at the Theatre Royal, Covent Garden . . .'

'And then we . . .'

'Ooh. Do you know, I think I left them in my dinki-doodi-den . . .'

'Oh, no, Bartlemas!'

'I'll scurry up and get them straight away.'

There was a brief pause. Nobody quite liked to ask what Bartlemas's dinki-doodi-den was. Fortunately he scurried back before the silence became awkward.

'Here it is, acres of bills and things.'

Gerald assumed control and looked through the papers while the others watched. Then he chuckled. 'The old sod.'

'Who?' asked Jacqui.

'Marius Steen. He'd really got it in for Nigel. He must have regretted that gift business.'

'Why? What did he do?' asked Charles.

'Marius wrote a letter to his son last November—this is a copy of it—complaining in humble terms about how he'd left himself short by the gift and not taken inflation into account, and would Nigel let him have a small income from various shares and properties? And here's the agreement duly signed by Nigel.'

'And what does it mean?'

'It means that Marius was retaining a beneficial interest in the gift.'

'What?' asked Jacqui blankly, which saved the embarrassment of someone else's asking.

'It means that the whole gift thing was invalid. Nigel would have had to pay duty on the whole estate without reduction.'

'Good God,' said Charles. 'You can't help admiring the old bugger. Making his own son sign away his fortune.'

'Yes. He was an amazing character. He understood

money,' said Gerald with respect, 'and, having made one mistake, determined that most of it would die with him.'

'Will it affect my inheritance?' Jacqui asked anxiously.

'Ah, who knows?' Gerald smiled. 'That all has to be sorted out by solicitors and accountants.'

Charles gave a mock yawn. 'I know. Endless meetings, confabulations, discussions and mumblings about the law. Where does all that get you?'

'Rich,' said Gerald smugly.

At half past eleven, they all left the house to go to the April Fools' Midnight Matinée at the Parthenon. Bartlemas and O'Rourke had dressed in their Victorian first-night gear specially. They looked like a pair of Dickensian undertakers.

The bright young theatrical crowd (including Gerald, who had decided he would go after all) piled into Bernard Walton's Bentley, leaving Charles and Joanne on the pavement outside the house. 'See you,' yelled Jacqui out of the window as the great car roared off.

'How've you been?' Charles asked Joanne.

'All right.'

'You still miss Marius?'

'Yes, but the new job's very busy, so it's not too bad.'

'Good. Do you fancy a drink somewhere?'

'Thanks very much, but no, I don't think so. I've got to be up early in the morning.'

Charles found a cruising taxi to take Joanne Menzies home. Then he hailed another for himself and gave the driver the address of the Montrose.